KATE CALLAGHAN

HOW MY DOG STOLE NEW YEAR'S

SNOW, MISTLETOE, AND MIDNIGHT KISSES AWAIT...

Mia Mulrooney has everything she could ever want: her thriving bakery, her cosy village, and a peaceful life free of August, the brooding guitarist who ghosted her two years ago on New Year's Eve.

But August is back in town for a New Year's wedding, and a fierce snowstorm traps them together for the weekend in Yule's oldest castle. As the storm rages outside, their undeniable chemistry ignites. Amid stolen kisses beneath twinkling mistletoe and whispered confessions in the dead of night, Mia's frozen heart begins to thaw. Yet, as midnight approaches, she must confront her feelings: can she forgive him and find the courage to let love back into her life?

HOW MY EX STOLE NEW YEAR'S

HOW MY EX STOLE NEW YEAR'S
KATE CALLAGHAN

Edited By Emma O' Connell

ISBN: 978-1-916684-28-7

First Edition 2025

www.callaghanwriter.com

OTHER BOOKS BY THE AUTHOR

YA Dark Fantasy | A Hellish Fairytale Series
Crowned A Traitor I
Where Traitors Fall II
When Traitors Rise III

Towerwood | Novella
Stepmother | Novella

Village of Yule | Stand-Alone Series
The Naughty Or Nice Clause
Tis The Season For Secrets
How My Ex Stole New Years

Village of FoxFord | Stand-Alone Series
Potions & Proposals
Don't Go Baking My Heart

Dangerous Harmonies | Stand-Alone Series
Ms Perfectly Fine
Not Another Rockstar
The Situation Ship

MIA & AUGUST PLAYLIST

Is It New Year's Yet? | Sabrina Carpenter
Lover | Taylor Swift
Love Of My Life | Harry Styles
Lights Down Low | MAX
Back To Decemeber | Taylor Swift
Ghost Of You | 5 seconds Of summer
Imagine | Ariana Grande
Revolving Door | Tate Mcrae
Maybe Don't | Maisie Peters
I Wanna Be Yours | Artic Monkeys

Scan Me

GLOSSARY

Technically, you don't have to read the other books in the series to enjoy Mia and August's story. However, here's a cheat sheet for the few bits you missed or need to be reminded of since we last ventured to Yule.

Yule/North Pole: A magical village set in a protected area of the North Pole.

Gold Bells: Ringing the bell causes the ringer to be magically transported to Yule. Only those who believe in Christmas will be able to use it.

Guardians of Yule: Those who help citizens of Yule live away from the village and adjust to the outside world, should they wish to leave Yule. They also make sure the secrecy of Yule is protected and maintained at all costs.

Council of Yule: The oldest families of Yule help run the village. The Klaus family are the most powerful, as the eldest son, Mason Klaus, is the current Santa Klaus.

KATE CALLAGHAN

HOW MY EX STOLE NEW YEAR'S

A VILLAGE OF YULE NOVELLA

New Years Past

Mia checked her watch repeatedly, waiting for the band to arrive as she stood behind the buffet table laden with hors d'oeuvres and desserts. However, most of the guests paid more attention to the bar and the complimentary champagne than to the food.

"Stop checking your watch, you're starting to verge on obsession," Michelle whispered, nudging her twin sister. With their hair slicked back, even if Michelle stuck to their natural copper while Mia's was peroxide blonde and pink-tipped, they were perfect copies of one another: green eyes and warm, pale skin that turned bright pink at the slightest increase in blood pressure. She could thank her Irish ancestry for that. "The fan meet will end soon, and then you'll have August all to yourself."

It was Brothers of Anarchy's final European concert in

Paris, and Michelle's catering company had been hired for the afterparty. In the lull between Christmas and New Year's, all the guests were either in the mood to party or nursing hangovers. Mia was happy to assist with desserts, even if she was technically breaking Yule law by being here, since she hadn't applied for her guardianship papers. Still, what the council of Yule – the secret village in the heart of the North Pole – didn't know wouldn't hurt them.

"I'm not obsessed!" Mia blushed, fixing the platter of cupcakes so they were aligned with the hors d'oeuvres. Usually, she'd play with her hair when she was anxious, but since it was tucked up in a low bun, she had to do something with her hands. Unfortunately, her twin sister could read her like a book. "I just wish I could be there for him. He loves his fans, but he hates the Q&As and being put on the spot. At least Axel is with him to make it easier. August's the silent type; he doesn't like to speak unless he absolutely has to."

Mia was lucky enough to be one of the few people outside of his band that he'd opened up to. This time last year, they'd met at Yule in her bakery, Sweet Pastries, on Candy Cane Lane. With August having lived on the Outside all his life, they never would have met if he hadn't come back for the festive season to visit his grandparents. He'd fallen in love with her mint chocolate éclairs, and she had fallen in love with the rugged and irresistibly awkward guitarist.

"Your obsession works for me; otherwise, I would've had to pay another waiter to help me out tonight," Michelle teased. "But I'm surprised you were able to leave your bakery. This is the crazy season in Yule – you must be exhausted. I'd have thought you'd be far too busy with catering orders for all the departments celebrating another successful Christmas Eve."

Mia suspected that August had suggested hiring her sister's catering company so they could see each other sooner, but she kept that thought to herself. It was a win-win for everyone. Her sister was an incredibly talented chef, while Mia was happy with her small bakery. Together, they were a dream team in the kitchen. Michelle had hoped they'd open a restaurant one day, but Yule was Mia's home. Michelle had always dreamed of more – of finding her own path, not an easy thing to do as a twin from a small, isolated village with a total population of 25,000. Mia was always happy to support her in that endeavour.

"I've hired some extra help this year, so I'm able to sneak away more often. Travelling by bell makes it much simpler to move back and forth without being noticed. Especially when I'm visiting August – the bell helps me get in and out of places without the press seeing me." Mia kept her voice low. Yule's number one rule was that no outsiders could ever discover the truth about the village's existence.

"Good point – the last thing you need is the paps looking into the mystery woman August is dating. I can imagine the headlines: *August Reid dating woman who doesn't even exist*. No birth certificate, no passport – they'd probably think he was holding you against your will, or that you're some secret spy."

"And my deadly weapon is a piping bag," Mia chuckled, making light of the serious problem. If she was caught outside without completing the guardianship programme in Yule to obtain her proper papers and cover Yule's trail, she could face banishment from the only home she'd known. She shook off those thoughts, as she had many times over the past year.

"Are you sure the risk is worth it? You love Yule and your quiet life in the bakery. He's the opposite," Michelle pointed out, the humour in her tone slipping away.

"If you had told me a year ago that I'd be risking everything for a man, I'd have called you crazy, but he *is* worth it. Loving him is worth it. If everything goes to plan, we won't have to keep our relationship a secret for much longer. He doesn't buy into the fame, and he leads a quiet life when he isn't touring. He loves music; his band is his family. I would never want him to stop, the same way he would never want me to give up the bakery."

"And you think you can make it work? He's on the Outside in one of the world's biggest rock bands, and you're at the North Pole?"

Mia wondered how long she had been hiding her concerns. They rarely got to see each other since Michelle had moved to the Outside five years ago, so maybe this was just her first chance to voice them.

"You know I like August – hell, I'm more a fan of the band than you are – but I'm scared you're falling so hard, and I don't want to see you get your heart broken," Michelle admitted.

"Trust me, I'm well aware of the obstacles. We've survived the last year – between my job in Yule and his touring, we take what we can get. We make it work. It's been two weeks since we last saw each other, and tonight is the perfect opportunity to see him in public without the press sniffing around. Please don't worry so much. After tonight, we're headed back to Yule and we're going to spend New Year's together before Brothers of Anarchy moves on to the US leg of their tour. I'm going to apply for my guardianship papers… and we're going to ask the council of Yule to give their blessing for our relationship." Mia noted her sister's visible sigh of relief at the confession.

"Are you getting engaged?" Michelle squealed, and a partygoer browsing the cupcakes grimaced in their direction, as if the staff were meant to be seen and not heard. As though her sister wasn't a Michelin-starred chef at the age of only twenty-eight!

Mia swatted at her. "I don't know if we're there yet. We haven't discussed it, but I'm hoping he's open to the idea – the council will be more open to our relationship if we're engaged. Either way, since he has Yule ancestry and I'm a citizen, we should be fine."

"You are totally getting engaged." Michelle beamed, clinging to her arm excitedly. "Are you going to introduce him to Mum and Dad?"

"He's planning on staying in Yule for most of January with me, so we're bound to run into each other. I don't want him to feel any pressure. Mum and Dad will lecture us about the distance and the band's notoriety. I don't even know if I'm ready to get engaged, but I can't imagine life without him either."

"They'll have questions for sure, but once they see how happy you are, I'm sure they'll approve. You're a grown woman, you're well able to decide for yourself – but I do absolutely insist on catering the wedding." Michelle winked. In spite of her own concerns, she would always be in her sister's corner.

"Can you please stop talking about weddings? I'm not getting engaged!" Mia whined, not wanting to get her hopes up. She decided to focus on replenishing the chocolate and lemon tarts on the silver trays. "No word of this when he arrives. No hints or mentions of rings, wedding bells, nothing—" Her phone buzzed in her back pocket.

"My lips are sealed. No jinxing the happy couple." Michelle grinned.

August: In the lift.

STRAIGHT TO THE POINT, no fluff, as always.

Mia: I'll be outside on the balcony when you want me.

August: I've spent the last two weeks wanting you.

"I know that look – lover boy has arrived." Michelle interrupted Mia smiling to herself like an idiot. "Don't you get tired of having to sneak around? Or does it make it all the more exciting?"

"Stop it! Maybe it adds a little excitement."

"You should have registered for Outside papers years ago! It's only filling in a few forms. Your assigned guardian only checks in periodically to ensure you're following the rules and that your documentation is up to date. Being with August wouldn't be as big a deal; we'd see more of each other, and you could get a driving licence."

"You just want to be the passenger princess for once. I might not be able to drive a car, but no one drives a sleigh better than I can," Mia chuckled, having no desire to get behind the wheel on the Outside. She lived within walking distance to everything important in Yule, and anywhere else she could hail a sleigh taxi. "I only leave Yule to see you. The bakery keeps me busy, and the big, wide world was never for me."

"Not anymore." Michelle nudged her, indicating to August, watching her from the other side of the room. He had cut his hair since they'd last met; the sides were shaved, showing the spiral tattoo on his ear, though some dark curls still topped his head.

Mia grabbed her coat and purposefully walked out through the glass doors to the balcony. As she passed August, she caught his wink, and she knew he would be right behind her.

In the chilly December air, she snugly wrapped her jacket around her, grateful to leave behind the loud music and rowdy crowd. When she looked back, August was nowhere to be seen among the band members in the crowd. She checked her phone to see if she had missed a message.

"Mind if I join you?" August asked, suddenly at her side.

Mia jumped, dropping her phone, but he caught it. She admired his reflexes, though the screen was already cracked.

"Good catch," she said quickly, holding herself back from jumping into his arms. August stepped closer, but she tilted her head toward the guests at the other end of the long balcony to remind him that they weren't alone. Instead, he stood by her side, overlooking the glittering city.

"My phone?" she asked, and he handed it to her. His fingers lingered on hers for a moment, revealing calluses from years of playing bass and guitar. She'd missed his hands; such a simple touch shouldn't make her feel so dizzy.

"I can have the screen fixed," he said, scratching the back of his head as they continued their charade of a polite conversation. Mia's eyes slid to the tears in his T-shirt, revealing the muscles beneath. Two weeks was far too long. "I didn't mean to frighten you. I just wanted to get away from the chaos inside."

"You're not enjoying the party?" Mia asked, making herself glance away.

"I prefer the view out here," he replied, his voice low.

Mia rolled her eyes, though she loved this side of him. With everyone else, he barely spoke; most people saw him as cold and distant, unreadable, and they would never believe how charming he could be, or guess at the sense of humour he kept buried under his social discomfort.

When she glanced at him, he was staring at her, not the breathtaking view. Inching closer, she almost gave in to the temptation to kiss him. The interruption of the other very drunk party-goers on the balcony spotting August forced her out of her trance before it was too late.

She slipped into the background, avoiding attention as the fans spoke *at* August.

Waiting for them to take the hint, she snagged a pineapple cupcake from a waiter's passing tray, smirking at how August merely nodded along to what they were saying. His eyes followed Mia's every movement as he leaned against the railing. She wondered if they even noticed he hadn't uttered a word before they congratulated him on a great show and went back inside.

"I thought you were quitting," Mia said, watching him remove a pack of cigarettes from his pocket and pop one between his lips.

"Since you won't let me kiss you in public, I need something to distract me and to keep me out here talking with a beautiful, talented baker," he said, fidgeting with his lighter, but he didn't light it.

Mia removed the golden foil surrounding the base of the cupcake before taking a bite.

"My God, have you tried these? Sometimes I'm surprised by my own talents," she said appreciatively, licking the icing from the corner of her lower lip.

August's eyes widened, and Mia watched him swallow as she licked her lips. She had never felt so sexy, having a devastatingly handsome, introverted rockstar transfixed simply by her eating a pineapple punch cupcake.

Without warning, August took her hand and bit into the rest of the cupcake. She gaped.

"I really have to give you a lesson in subtlety." Mia chuckled as his eyes rolled back in his head.

"You can teach me anything you like," he said, licking the icing from the corner of his mouth where the ring piercing had caught some. "It's a pity these are wasted on the drunks."

"Stop it, you're making me blush." She didn't know how much longer she could stand to be so close to him without touching him. "Thank you, but it doesn't matter to me whether they're drunk or not, so long as the cakes are enjoyed." She sighed, wiping more icing from her lip and sucking on her thumb. "I'd better call it a night."

August clenched his jaw, and she knew he was close to breaking. She crumbled up the cupcake foil and placed it in his hand.

"So soon?" he groaned, leaning in closer – too close. Mia couldn't help the way her breath caught.

"I've been here for four hours already, helping my sister," she said, walking past him, lingering a little too long. "You were late."

"Sorry for keeping you waiting," he whispered. "Cillian and Nick got carried away with the encores, but I would've much preferred to be here. With you."

"Forgiven – but I'm afraid if I don't go, I might blow our cover," she told him quietly, backing away from him.

"I'm not ready to say goodbye." He followed her, his fingertips brushing hers subtly. "Let me come with you?"

"Why would you want to leave all this?" Mia teased, looking around the packed room, full of people there to celebrate him and his band's tour.

"Because I'm craving something sweet?" August winked, holding the door open for her. Mia found it hard to resist his delicious smile, knowing his lips would taste of sweet and tangy frosting.

"I already gave you the rest of my cupcake."

"It's not enough. I'm still hungry."

"Then… I think we should get out of here." Mia diverted her gaze, removed her hotel key card from her pocket, and pretended to bump into him so she could slip it into his pocket without raising suspicion. In the crowd of guests, his hand brushed her lower back. She playfully swatted him away but still felt his eyes on her as she walked off. She added a little shimmy to her step to hold his attention as she headed towards the kitchen to find Michelle.

"Your cheeks are so red," Michelle giggled, organising the next round of platters.

"Probably just the cold." Mia placed her free hand on her warm cheek, embarrassed about the effect he had on her blood pressure.

"Thank you for reminding me just how single I am," Michelle whined. "You're making me jealous. I take it you're heading out?"

Mia winced, grabbing her things. "Sorry to cut and run—"

"Go! If I had a sexy hunk waiting for me, I wouldn't even hesitate to abandon you." Michelle gave her a tight squeeze before letting her go.

She'd expected August to meet her at the hotel room, but as the lift doors were about to close, a hand shot out between them. August's devilish grin greeted her, and he slid in beside her. He kept enough distance between them to avoid suspicion, but his hand grazed hers by her side, and she played with his fingers, intertwining hers with his.

The door closed, and Mia's cheeks flushed as August caught her glancing at him. Her mind swirled with wild thoughts of everything she'd wanted him to do with her over the past two weeks. She had missed everything about him – his lips, eyes, hands, and even the scent of his cologne. The tension that had been growing since she'd felt him standing behind her on the balcony finally overwhelmed her. She couldn't bear another moment apart from his embrace.

Her heart quickened as she entered his space, pinning him against the wall. August smirked, his dark eyes tempting and enticing her as she ran her hands down his chest.

"Fuck it," he breathed, his voice deep and low with desire that made her toes curl.

Mia rose on her toes to press her lips to his, then started to pull back. His arm quickly encased her, pulling her closer, and he returned her kiss – deep, passionate, and fuelled by a raw need that made her heart race. His lips gently coaxed hers open, and the scent of cigarette smoke and mint overwhelmed her senses. She was desperate to be closer to him. Her hands found his dark hair, gripping it as if she never wanted to let go. He tilted his head, making it easier for her to reach him, while his palm softly circled her back to soothe and reassure, his lips were possessive and demanding. Waves of pleasure made her knees weak, causing her to forget their surroundings.

A sharp *bing* forced them apart, signalling they'd arrived at their floor. August drew back so quickly that he banged his head against the back of the wall. His obvious frustration made Mia giggle. She cleared her throat, concealing her amusement as she headed into the hallway a few paces ahead of him, so it didn't look like they were going to the same place.

Just as she reached the hotel room, a couple stopped August for a picture. Opening the door, Mia glanced over her shoulder and winked as the couple kept him from her. He shook his head, his eyes narrowing, telling her she was going to pay for her teasing later.

"GOOD MORNING," August said softly, brushing Mia's hair out of her face as she struggled to open her eyes.

"Where are you off to? The sun isn't even up yet," she asked, snuggling the duvet under her chin. Outside the window, it was still dark, but he was already getting dressed and smelling of cedarwood and toothpaste. She'd been so wiped out she hadn't heard him get up or shower. "It's chilly in this large bed without you."

"I've a meeting with our manager and the guys for breakfast, but I'll see you back at your bakery in Yule tonight. I've ordered you breakfast, so sleep in, and I'll take care of the room," he said, pressing his lips to her forehead.

His grandparents must have given him a Yule bell when he saw them at Christmas. "Are you sure? Don't we need to check out?"

"Not until eleven, and it's only seven."

"You're spoiling me," Mia groaned, leaning up on her elbows. She watched him pull on his tattered T-shirt, disappointed as she saw his lean muscles disappear beneath the black, bleached fabric. She wanted to pull him back into bed, but he shouldn't miss his meeting, and she didn't think her body could handle another round.

"I hope so. I'll see you tonight, and we'll enjoy two weeks of uninterrupted bliss – no crowds, fans, or interruptions," August promised.

"Are you sure you want to be away from your friends for New Year's? I'd understand if you want to come back and spend some time with them," Mia said, trying not to pressure him. The prospect of being together with him in Yule, meeting with the council, and facing the first real test of their relationship sent a shiver of concern down her spine. When they'd first met, August even maintaining eye contact for a complete sentence was rare. Now that she had all of him, she was afraid that the wall might come back down between them. He knew her fears but had promised not to disappear, and he had kept that promise so far, and more.

"Are you kidding? I've already told them I need some alone time, and they understand. They don't know that my alone time now includes you. I don't want to waste a single second before we're apart again for three months. Besides, we need to get your guardianship papers sorted, because I'm not going through another tour without being able to see you. No more hiding. Soon you'll be stuck with me forever," he teased.

His words sounded a lot like a proposal, sending butterflies through her tummy. She loved how open he was about missing her and how much he wanted to be with her.

"I'd be honoured." Blushing, she sat up and wrapped

her arms around his neck, loving how his eyes widened in surprise as she pressed her lips firmly against his, pouring all her desire and love into a silent message. She was all in, his, with or without a proposal.

"You're making it impossible for me to leave," he said against her lips as he fisted the band T-shirt she was wearing.

"Fine," she breathed playfully. "Leave before I'm tempted to lock you up in this room."

"I can be late," he said gruffly, holding her tight against him as if she might float away.

"No, you can't," she chuckled. "Just see it as a preview for tonight."

After a muffled protest and a soft shove from Mia, August got off the bed, pouting as he slowly headed towards the front door. She blew him a kiss, and he caught it dramatically.

The door closed and she sank back onto the pillows, kicking her feet like a happy child, amazed at how fortunate she was to have found her person.

LATER THAT NIGHT IN YULE, Mia waited outside her bakery after closing, the snow falling around her, for August to arrive. An hour passed, and her hands were blue and her nose bright red as she stood under the pink awning, straining with the snow and icicles hanging from the edges.

She decided to go inside and wait, but another hour

passed, and the only people who passed her were late-night shoppers picking up belated Christmas presents for their loved ones. It wasn't odd for Yule citizens to celebrate after the fact, since it was their busiest work season.

Mia didn't know how long she sat on the stool by the front window, staring, waiting, holding her breath, only to be let down every time she heard footsteps in the pools of melting snow on the cobblestones. August never appeared.

Worried something might have happened, she tried to call him, but the number wouldn't work. Calling the Outside world from Yule could be unreliable; perhaps it wasn't connecting. Her text messages went undelivered.

Glancing at the clock above the coffee machine, she realised she had to get up to start preparing the pastries for the morning rush in an hour. August really wasn't coming; her eyes burned and her stomach knotted at the weight of reality crashing in on her. He'd broken his promise. She wrote a note for her customers, swallowed her tears, and attached it to the front door, struggling to keep herself upright because her legs were numb from sitting on the stool for so long.

CLOSED DUE TO UNFORESEEABLE CIRCUM-STANCES. REGULAR HOURS WILL RETURN AFTER NEW YEAR'S DAY.

Rumours would spread about her closing for a few days, but she was too heartbroken, too numb – if it was even possible to be both at once – to care. She went to bed in her small cottage, lit the fire beside her, and crawled under the covers, wishing the world would vanish or that she'd wake up and August would be beside her in bed, and this night would turn out to be nothing but a terrible nightmare.

Sinking into the mattress, Mia checked her phone over and over again, silently hoping he would call or text to explain. She told herself and her racing heart that she was overreacting, but no message arrived. She didn't understand what she had done wrong and cried herself to sleep after eating the eclairs she had made especially for him. How could so much have changed in a matter of hours? It wasn't like she could go looking for him; she didn't exist in the Outside, and she couldn't confront his bandmates without exposing Yule. She could do nothing but wait and see.

For days, Mia moved through her days on autopilot. There was no sign of him – no texts, calls, or messages. She even checked her email, since he had no social media except the Brothers of Anarchy band page, which only posted updates about upcoming gigs. Weeks went by, and as she served her cheerful customers, her forced smile became a habit.

Her only solace was that they were worlds apart, and she would never have to face him again.

New Year's Present
Two Years Later

After visiting his grandparents' townhouse and indulging in far too much of his grandmother's sherry trifle, August waited with his luggage at the candy-striped sleigh rank for a transfer to the castle-turned-hotel nestled deep in the woods of Yule. Given the never-ending night in the North Pole, it was easy to lose track of time, and he didn't want to be late checking in. Returning to Yule for his cousin Molly's wedding had provided a much-needed break following Brothers of Anarchy's latest album release. Heavy snow began to fall, so he flagged down a passing sleigh to ensure he wouldn't be late checking in.

"Evening, any chance you could take me up to the castle?" he asked the bearded sleigh driver, stroking the reindeer's nose. As always, August had told his bandmates he was going skiing for the New Year break; although he disliked lying to them, he did frequently ski in the mountains surrounding the village of Yule when visiting his grandparents.

"Sure, hop in. You don't mind sharing? I've a pickup booked, and you're both heading up to the castle anyway. With the snow coming down so hard, I don't want to leave her waiting," the driver explained, looking over his shoulder as he loaded August's luggage.

August hesitated, only to remember he didn't require security in Yule; no one in the village paid attention to his fame. They just thought of him as the reclusive grandson of the Reid family, who played in some band on the Outside. He was just like any other guest heading to his cousin's wedding on New Year's Eve. It also helped that fame was relatively meaningless in the town; all that mattered to the citizens was that the magical dust was delivered by the Klaus every year to families all over the world by Christmas Day. It was the one place August could be completely unbothered.

"Don't mind at all," he lied, putting his guitar case in the back before climbing into the seat behind the driver and pulling one of the fur blankets onto his lap. He didn't like strangers getting close to him, especially when it meant sharing a twenty-minute sleigh ride, but after spending most of the year on the Outside, adjusting to the cold was a bit challenging. He didn't know how long he might have to wait for another sleigh, especially on the Thursday before New Year's weekend.

"You coming in for the wedding? The whole castle has

been booked out for New Year's weekend. I'm sure the couple spent a pretty penny," the driver commented.

August doubted the castle, one of the oldest buildings in Yule, could accommodate all the guests. Yule weddings tended to be grand; in a place where so many knew each other, it was hard to limit invitations. His grandparents were helping to pay for some of it, since they had raised Molly after her parents died in a mining accident when she was a teenager. Molly was the relative August was closest to. As kids, she used to keep him company during the holidays. His parents had brought him to Yule to meet his extended family every year, and she was the only one who didn't judge him for his delayed speech and his freak-outs when people got too close.

"Yes," he said flatly, and the driver picked up on the cue not to continue the conversation.

A lump formed in his throat as they drove past Mia's bakery, Sweet Pastries. Nothing had changed; the same awning, the same gold cursive lettering on the front window. The lights were off, and he guessed she had closed early for the wedding. It had been two years since he'd left her, but not a day went by without him regretting it or missing her. He really wished he had stopped by the pub before heading to the castle; he'd thought he was more prepared to see her again than he actually was. Of all the people Molly could have ended up with, she *had* to marry Mia's twin sister, Michelle. He'd met Michelle at their engagement dinner last month, and she had been just as shocked to see him again.

August had been expecting a row, and he deserved it, but Michelle obviously hadn't wanted to spoil the night for Molly, so she was perfectly polite, even if he could tell he wasn't in her good books. She explained that Mia couldn't make it because she had the flu. August figured Michelle would have told her sister he would be attending the wedding, but his troubles didn't matter. This weekend was about Molly, not him and his mistakes. He'd do whatever he could to make this easier for Mia, even if it meant avoiding her as best he could. It wouldn't be easy, considering that he was the best man and she the maid of honour.

They headed along the main streets, and a sudden halt outside the small pale yellow cottage sent a cold shiver down his spine. Seeing the very person he'd been most afraid of encountering wrapped in an oversized black puffy coat and orange scarf with matching earmuffs, struggling with her bags as she closed the gate to her home, nearly stopped his heart.

His mind went blank, and he didn't know what to say to her. Apologise? Beg? Get out of the sleigh and let her travel alone? What he really wanted to do was wrap his arms around her and tell her how much he regretted leaving her, how he wanted to spend the rest of his days making it right – but he froze, his words lost to him.

"I'm glad you were running a little late. I couldn't find my dress bag, so I only just got out the door myself," Mia panted as August automatically took her bag and placed it on his lap so she could get herself seated. "Thank you. It's heavier than I thought."

"It's no trouble," the driver said, keeping the reindeer steady on the road. Before she slipped on the step up,

August reached out to catch Mia's hand. He hoped she wouldn't notice how much he was shaking.

"Thanks. The step is slippery." Mia smiled at him, embarrassed, and his heart threatened to stop as her warm expression changed to cold shock. Dread strangled him. Would she yell, cry, slap him and go back inside? He deserved all of it.

"Hi, Mia," he stammered, staring at the woman he'd ghosted two years ago after the best year of his life. *That's the best you can do? Hi?* He cursed himself.

"Hi, August."

Her cool indifference felt worse than a hard slap. August didn't know what he'd expected or hoped for, but there was no anger in her voice, only surprise. Apparently, Michelle hadn't warned her that he would be attending the wedding. He had hoped to speak to her before the ceremony to explain and apologise; ambushing her in a sleigh outside her home had certainly not been the plan. Mia looked as if she couldn't decide whether to sit down or run away. He had to admit he wouldn't blame her if she told him to leave.

"You two know each other?" the taxi driver said, looking between them, but neither answered. They just stared at each other, not knowing what else to say.

"We did, but it's been a while," Mia said at last, getting in.

August shifted and noticed her freeze, like he was a panther waiting to pounce.

"That works out well. Sharing with a stranger can be a little awkward, but I couldn't leave the poor man stranded in this heavy snow," the driver said, interrupting the tense moment.

"I can get out if you want me to. I don't want to make you uncomfortable," August offered quietly as Mia inched as far away from him as physically possible. Living in Yule her whole life, she would be accustomed to the cold, but it was a long drive. He reached for the spare blanket, and she snatched it before he could offer it.

"Why would you make me uncomfortable? We're both adults going to the same place, no need to make a fuss." She forced a smile, but didn't meet his eyes. He didn't press, not wanting to start an argument in front of the driver.

"How's the bakery going? My daughter is so grateful you took her on as an apprentice; every day, her mother and I wake up to pastries and cakes. If we aren't careful, she'll put us into sugar comas," the driver chuckled. The reindeer picked up speed once they passed the large, ornately decorated Christmas tree at the heart of the village and headed into the woods. August was grateful for his conversation. Anything to break the silence.

"Everything's going great, and there's no need to thank me. Sarah's talented and great with the customers. I'd be happy to take her on full-time when she finishes her final exams before she goes to pastry school. I know she has her heart set on studying in Germany," Mia said, now seemingly unbothered by or refusing to acknowledge his presence. August admired her composure; he was a second away from leaping out of the sleigh into the snow to avoid the tension between them.

"She'd love that. Have you visited Sweet Pastries?" the

driver asked August as they headed through the dense trees, enveloped in the smell of pine.

He attempted to put Mia at ease with a compliment. "Not for a long time, but it's hard to forget."

Judging by how pink she went, it had worked.

"You'll probably get another chance to visit the bakery while you're here."

"I'll be closed until after New Year's. Getting everything ready for my sister's wedding has been a feat, so I'm taking some time off afterwards," Mia sighed, fidgeting with her fluffy gloves.

"He'll get a chance to try your baking again at the wedding then – my daughter told me you're doing the wedding cake," the driver put in.

"Wedding? You're invited to the wedding?" Mia's head snapped towards August. "My sister invited you to her wedding?!"

"It's also my cousin's wedding. Where else would I be?" Why on earth hadn't Michelle and Molly given her a heads up? *Maybe they couldn't figure out a way to tell her.*

"You're Molly's cousin?" Mia shut her eyes and took a deep breath. "Your cousin is marrying my sister." It sounded more like she was letting the news sink in than addressing him.

"Sorry. I thought they would've told you that I'm the best man," he offered.

"What a coincidence," laughed the driver.

"*I* thought you would be busy with the band," Mia said coolly, looking out at the trees instead of at him. "Isn't Brothers of Anarchy meant to be headed to New York for the ball drop?" Even with the extra space between them, he could smell her perfume – a sweet citrus and vanilla scent that made him want to pull her close and not let her go again.

"I'm surprised you know what we're up to." He wondered if she had been keeping up to date with the band because she couldn't move on; he certainly hadn't. That meant she must know about everything that has happened recently. He hoped she wouldn't bring it up. He wanted to talk to her, to explain, but stuck in the back of a sleigh with the driver listening in didn't feel like the right time to talk about something so raw.

"That's the problem with fame – I couldn't avoid news about you even if I tried," she admitted. "Besides, your grandmother comes into the bakery and brags about her talented grandson every week."

"Sorry." The apology was long overdue, but he didn't know what he was apologising for: his grandmother, his abandoning her without a word two years ago, or having broken his promise not to break her heart. "Yes, they're performing on New Year's in New York."

"And you didn't want to go with them?" Mia asked, placing her bag between them as if she needed a physical barrier to keep them apart.

"I wasn't going to miss Molly's wedding; she's like a sister to me," he told her. "Birthdays, Christmas – I've missed a lot while I was touring."

"Mia's guilty of the same – can never get her away from the bakery. My wife even tried to set her up on some blind dates, but nothing comes between her and her bakery. If she wasn't responsible for the wedding cake, we doubt she'd even be attending."

"Argyle!" Mia snapped. Clearly, she and the old man knew each other well.

The thought of her going on blind dates made August's blood boil, but hearing she had refused gave him hope that she was still single. He couldn't ask outright; he didn't have the right to pry into her life. He'd given that up that night – the night he'd left her waiting.

"And where would your wife be getting her morning coffee on the way to the flower shop if I was out swanning around on dates? Baking is like breathing to me, so sacrificing a social life is worth it," Mia retorted. August knew the feeling.

"You love it, so it's worth the sacrifice. I feel the same about music," he said, watching the sparkle in her eyes. "Though it's risky to love something so deeply, isn't it? Sometimes the passion overwhelms us, and we abandon the people we care about in pursuit of it." He'd forgotten how easy it was to be around her. She was the only one he could talk to like this; around her, he found it hard to filter.

"I suppose, but I could never walk away from something I truly loved, not without good reason. You must really love Molly to leave the band for her."

Her loaded words struck him. They weren't talking about baking any longer. She thought he'd chosen the band over her, and she was right – but not in the way she believed, and he didn't have time to explain as they reached the driveway, its hedges decorated with fairy lights and snow.

An uncomfortable silence settled between them, as though an invisible wall separated them.

"I owe Molly. I wouldn't be in the band without her," August said suddenly, and Mia's eyes snapped to his. In the year they'd dated, he'd never told her how he discovered music. Part of him was still ashamed. "I suffered from intense anxiety when I was younger; my hands would shake constantly, worse when I was around others, and nothing would stop them. Then Molly gifted me a second-hand bass one Christmas." He held up his hand. "Steady as a rock. So... I'd never miss her wedding."

He wanted Mia to know he didn't walk away from those he loved. He'd never meant to abandon her, but so much had happened the day he'd left, and he couldn't drag her into his mess. Still, that was behind him now, and he needed her to understand that it hadn't happened because he didn't love her enough; it was because he'd wanted to protect her.

"I'm glad you were able to be so open about your struggles with her. That she helped you find your passion. I'm envious." Mia stared at him so fiercely that he felt like she was piercing his soul.

Before August could reply, a gardener shovelling the long driveway for the arriving guests swung the castle gates open. Despite their obvious efforts, it was a losing battle against the heavy snowfall. The sleigh arrived in front of the fairytale castle, crossing a long gravel path. It felt like an episode of Outlander – minus the kilts; the charm of Yule's historic buildings was timeless. The exterior featured two large Christmas trees, decorated with twinkling lights, which perfectly fitted the holiday theme. Since Yule's busiest season was Christmas, the brides had chosen New Year's as the perfect occasion to celebrate their favourite season and welcome the new year.

"Let me help you down," August offered, reaching for Mia's dress bag as she struggled with it and her suitcase.

"I'm fine," Mia snapped, grabbing her things once they stopped in front of the steps. He didn't get a chance to say goodbye before she hurried up the red carpeted steps and through the arched doorway, where a grey-suited butler waited inside the tall grey stone building to take her bags and hand her a glass of champagne.

This is going to be a long weekend, August thought, sinking back in his seat and tugging his cap on and off in frustration. He paid Argyle and took a few moments to smoke a cigarette, giving Mia some space to check in without him lurking close by.

Don't *throw up, don't throw up!* Mia repeated silently to herself once she got away from August. Her stomach had been in a tight knot from the moment she saw him sitting in the sleigh. He had the same handsome smile, but there was a fear in his eyes she hadn't seen before. Was he afraid to see her, or just scared of her reaction? She'd been in such a state of shock that she was amazed at how civil she'd remained.

For two years, she had gone over and over in her mind what she would do or say if she ever saw him again, but seeing him sitting there, it felt like a lifetime had passed, yet also no time at all. She hadn't realised until now that beneath the shock and anger, there was a hint of excitement, maybe even relief – that she might get answers at last. Closure.

Mia downed her flute of champagne and unzipped her jacket, stifled by the heat inside the castle thanks to the fires in every corner. She took a breath as she reached the front desk, decorated with gold tinsel and red suede ribbons. Glancing behind her, she checked that August hadn't followed her in, but she would see him again soon either way, so she had to gather her senses and composure quickly before she fell apart. He wasn't going to see her cry, panic or squirm; she wouldn't give him the satisfaction of knowing his mere presence still affected her. *Why wouldn't Michelle have told me about his connection to Molly? Why would she not tell me he was not only coming to the wedding but was the best man?* It wasn't like her sister to keep secrets, and this wasn't just a secret, but a bomb.

"Ms Mulrooney, did you hear me?" The receptionist in her maroon suit smiled politely.

"No, sorry, I was a million miles away. I think my brain froze in the snow. You mentioned something about the weather?" Mia asked, not wanting to appear rude.

"I'm sorry for the inconvenience, but due to the snowstorm, we've had many guests unable to check out because their homes have lost power. We're asking all wedding guests if they wouldn't mind doubling up?"

"Oh. I'll stay at home and come back for the rehearsal dinner and the wedding," Mia said, not wanting to share a room with a stranger. She could easily get a taxi back and forth, even if it would be a bit of an inconvenience.

"Are you sure?" the receptionist asked anxiously. She'd clearly had a rough day dealing with guests.

"Ignore my maid of honour. Of course she'll be staying," Michelle said, draping her arm around her sister's shoulder. Mia opened her mouth to argue, but Michelle tutted. "It's my wedding, so no arguing with the bride. They've been working so hard to make sure the snow doesn't ruin our plans! Thankfully, we've been able to solve most of the issues so far, and it's forecast to blow over by tomorrow afternoon. You're my maid of honour, so I need you with me for all the events, and you still have to finish the cake. If it continues to snow like this, then you might not be able to get back here," she reasoned, snatching the room key for her sister.

Mia groaned. "Do I at least get to pick who I'm sharing with?"

"I'm sorry, but since you're one of the last to arrive, there's only one room left allocated for the wedding, and two of you to check in."

"That will teach you to arrive early."

"Don't worry, dear sister, nothing could stop me from getting here." Mia forced herself to smile, though she wished she had booked her own room in advance instead of just adding her name to the list for rooms the hotel had allocated for the wedding party. Spending time with August had made the drive to the castle seem so much longer. She couldn't believe how much she'd babbled about her baking. He had been looking at her so intently, as though reading her every thought; she couldn't stop herself from waffling on. "I would've been here earlier, but I had to drop off your cake this morning and then pick up my bridesmaid dress from the seamstress, since you wanted the hemline a quarter-inch shorter."

"I'm precise, sue me, and you're here now – that's all that matters. I want everything to be perfect. You can't refuse your twin on her wedding weekend, and nobody was expecting a snowstorm. You know the castle is the first place for people living in the woods to shelter during storms, so the only choice was to cancel the wedding until next year or double up." Michelle pouted and fluttered her eyelashes.

"Fine, I'll stay," Mia said, and the receptionist motioned for the butler to take her bags up to room 124. Michelle had spent a year planning the wedding; Mia wasn't going to give the bride any extra problems. Besides, she wanted to give her an inch before she confronted her twin about August's surprise appearance.

"How was the ride here?" Michelle said, taking Mia's arm as they headed for the gold lift. Yule's historical society, which oversaw maintaining and restoring Yule's most important historical sites, had allowed the lift to be added a few years ago when the castle was repurposed into a hotel so that the castle would be accessible to everyone.

"It was fine, but speaking of sharing, I wasn't alone on my journey here."

"Really? Must be a sleigh shortage with the weather," Michelle mused, hitting the button.

"Aren't you going to ask who I was sharing with?"

"How would I know?"

"Because he's a guest at your wedding. Someone critical to your bride, in fact. Can't have a wedding without your maid of honour, but you know who else you can't be without?" Mia ground out.

"Best man." Michelle sighed. "You know about August. In my defence, I only realised who he was at the engagement party."

"Know about him? I just spent twenty minutes in a sleigh with the man I haven't seen in two years, and who *you've* known would be attending for over a month!"

"I'm so sorry – please don't be mad at me. I should've told you. I was as clueless as you were when he appeared at the engagement party. Molly knew he had dated *a* Mia, but he didn't like to talk about it, so we didn't put the pieces together. He and Molly don't share the same last name." Michelle never liked to confront uncomfortable topics; she didn't see the point of arguing when there was a perfectly good rug to sweep everything under. If it weren't for the wedding, Mia would have given her a good lecture, but now wasn't the time.

"I understand that it's important to Molly to have him here, and I wouldn't have made you choose between us. This is your wedding, and I want you to be happy. I just wish you had given me some warning."

"I swear on my life that I was going to tell you when you arrived, but with all the snow chaos and getting everything ready, I was afraid you'd be angry and not come, and I really need you here with me. You're half of me, and I can't do this weekend without you."

"I'm not going anywhere. If he's uncomfortable, then he can leave," Mia reasoned.

"You're really okay with him being here?"

"It's been two years, and yes, it was a shock, but I'm over him," Mia lied – to both her sister and herself. "I'm sure I can handle some polite conversation."

"You're a better woman than me; I'd be a mess or murderous," Michelle chuckled, but the concern in her eyes was unmistakable. "Feel free to avoid him as much as possible, and don't worry – you'll be so busy with the bachelorette and the wedding itinerary that you won't even notice he's here."

I very much doubt that. Mia kept the thought to herself.

"But please, no more surprises," she groaned, selecting the button for the fourth floor.

"Not a single one, I promise." Michelle crossed her heart and kissed her sister's cheek. "And if you need to talk, please come to our suite, we're foregoing the separate rooms before the wedding. Even if you say you're fine, I know how much he meant to you."

The more Mia thought about August, the more her heart pounded, so she changed the subject. "This weekend isn't about me and him, it's about you and Molly. Actually, most importantly, it's about your cake. The tiers are safely in the freezer and ready to be put together on Saturday."

"I saw, and I'm so excited to see the completed masterpiece. Molly's so obsessed with the little figurines you made of us! You really went above and beyond." Michelle beamed. Her excitement was infectious.

Mia had delivered the tiers of white chocolate and vanilla cake this morning so that she wouldn't risk damaging it. The raspberry buttercream, edible chocolate flowers, and cake toppers had been packed separately so that the cake would be as fresh as possible on Sunday. Thinking of the cake helped relax her. Anything to focus on other than the man only a few floors below, who'd crushed her heart as easily as a meringue.

"I promised you the wedding cake of your dreams, and it really will be my crowning jewel. You should be happy I'm letting you cut it up. Only for my sister and her beautiful bride." Mia wrapped her arm around her sister, determined to focus on her. "Has Mum got drunk yet and started oversharing childhood stories? Is Dad freaking out about the snow?"

"Molly is ensuring the champagne remains corked until the bachelorette tonight. Although the bar in the lounge has discounted the drinks due to the inconvenience of the storm. It's going to get very tipsy very quickly, but as long as the guests are happy, I don't care. Our wedding planner has the patience of a saint and answers Dad's every question," Michelle said. "Besides, if Mum and Dad are tipsy, then they'll leave my staff alone. Why did both our parents have to be chefs?"

"Because we needed to inherit their talents," Mia said, proud of her sister for running the castle kitchen as executive chef for over a year now.

"True, but it also means they love to micro-manage."

"So that's where you got it from?" They reached the fourth floor and stepped out. "How is Molly doing, anyway? This can't be easy without her parents."

"It was hard at first. She really wishes her parents were here. I think that's why it's so important to her to have August and both sets of her grandparents. Mum and Dad have really stepped up. Mum helped her pick her dress, and Dad's going to walk her down the aisle."

"Who's going to walk you down the aisle?"

"Who else but my dearest sister?" Michelle said, reaching the room.

"I'd be honoured," Mia beamed, instantly teary-eyed, though giving her away felt like giving away half of herself.

"Good. Now, settle in, and please don't be late for the bachelorette. East Wing Ballroom: Molly is holding hers in the West Ballroom, so you won't have to see *him*, and I refuse to lose you to her." Michelle winked.

"Don't worry, I'm all yours this evening," Mia said, ushering her to the door. "And the sooner you leave, the sooner I can get ready!" She closed the door behind her twin, wanting to settle in before her roommate arrived.

"If you need anything, Molly and I are in the honeymoon suite on the sixth floor, in the west wing," Michelle called through the door, before her footsteps disappeared back down the hall.

Finally alone with her thoughts, Mia kicked off her shoes and felt the cold air flowing around her feet through the gap between the new carpet and the old, rustic door. Luckily, the butler who'd dropped off her bags had lit the small fire in the corner, and it was burning nicely, so it should quickly warm the room. Mia glanced at the clock on the fireplace adorned with silver tinsel and realised she had very little time before tonight's bachelorette party.

Only one bed. Great. She didn't want to share a bed with someone she had never met before. She could negotiate with her surprise roommate about who would get the bed and who would get the small couch by the balcony doors.

Heading into the bathroom, she ran the bath, hoping to wash away August's return and start afresh. *I can handle him. It's only four days, and then he'll be gone for good,* she told herself in the mirror. She wished she'd had more sleep last night; the dark circles beneath her green eyes needed plenty of concealer. She had stayed up late, deepcleaning the bakery, since she didn't want to return to expired food or a smelly kitchen. At least she'd found time to have her roots touched up, as the mousy brown had been starting to show through her honey blonde, though she'd chopped the pink ends for the wedding photos. The damp hadn't helped with the frizz. This was not how she'd wanted August to see her for the first time; if she ever ran into him again, she wanted to look flawless, not a frizzy, exhausted, tongue-tied mess.

Stripping off, she stepped into the scorching water and bubbles, soon to be relaxed and ready to head back downstairs. Unbothered and unfazed by her ex.

August

"You didn't tell Mia that I was coming?" August asked, finding Molly in the lounge bar, organising the seating chart for the rehearsal dinner.

"Michelle promised me she was going to tell her, but it must've slipped through the cracks. Besides, we aren't getting involved in the mess you made. You need to apologise and play nice, because if you ruin this weekend or upset Mia, then I'll leave you out in the storm to freeze to death." Molly grinned at him, tucking her pen into her dark curls, pinned up in a bun.

"I'm not here to cause any trouble, and the last thing I want is to hurt Mia any more than I already have." August ran his hand through his hair. "I'm not the only surprise this weekend. When I checked in, I learned that she agreed to share a room with me."

Molly's head snapped around. "Are you out of your mind? Did you plan this?"

"No. I can be blamed for a lot of things, but not the weather, and it was you who refused to cancel the wedding, so we're following your wishes and doubling up."

"Right… I just didn't expect that you'd end up in the same room."

"You heard, then?" Michelle said, coming up behind him.

"Michelle, good to see you."

"Wish I could say the same, but I think all three of us are to blame for not warning Mia. I think if you two can keep your distance and be pleasant, then we should be alright," Michelle sighed, clearly having spoken to Mia. He might not be her favourite person, but at least she didn't hate him outright, or at least not that she showed. He got the impression she tolerated him for Molly's sake, and he didn't blame her.

"Don't worry, darling, I've already threatened to have him sleep out in the snow if he upsets Mia," Molly said, kissing her fiancée.

"Another reminder of why I love you so much." Michelle smiled, reaching out for the seating chart, but Molly swatted away her hand.

"Don't even think about it. I've just got everyone placed perfectly."

"I should know better than to question you," giggled Michelle.

"Can you be all loved-up somewhere else? I'm trying to drink away my anxiety," August groaned. If his plan had come to fruition, it would've been his wedding to Mia they were attending, but clearly fate had had other plans.

The burn in his chest from the expensive vodka was a welcome distraction.

"No, you can't get drunk yet. You've to attend my bachelorette party later, and I want you to pass out at a reasonable hour, as tradition dictates."

He put down his vodka and stepped away from the bar. "I'm counting down the seconds, but first I need to go and freshen up."

"Not so fast! You promised to show me your suits when you arrived," Molly said, stopping him in his tracks.

"How could I forget? You have a navy and black to pick from." August placed his suit bag on the table.

"I think the navy would go nicely with the lilac bridesmaid dresses—"

"But black might be safer," Michelle chimed in, "unless you want the best man to stand out."

"Not really your colour, is it?" Molly asked, removing a lilac bridesmaid dress from the bag.

"Where's my suit? I had it in the sleigh…" August groaned. He'd been so distracted by Mia, they must have switched garment bags on the way.

"Please tell me you didn't forget your suit for my wedding. I love you, but I think I'll kill you if you wear sweats and a band T-shirt to the ceremony," Molly said, only half-joking.

August ran his hands through his hair. "Mia has it."

"Mia? Why would Mia have your suit?" Molly asked, confused.

"Because we shared a sleigh to get here – our dress bags must have got mixed up. I'll head to our room and get them for your approval."

"You're sharing a room with Mia? My sister?" Michelle's voice pitched in panic. "Does she know this? I just left her in the room, and I don't think she knows you're her new roommate."

"The receptionist said she had agreed to share because of the lack of rooms." August shrugged, but Michelle didn't look convinced.

"She's a better woman than I am. If I'd been brutally ghosted, I'd make you sleep outside in the snow and burn your suit," Molly chuckled, only to wince at his reaction.

"Thank you for that. I'm well aware of the pain I caused her, and I've no plans or desire to make this weekend any harder than it has to be," August snapped. He didn't know what was worse – Mia hating him, or having no feelings towards him at all.

"I don't care about the suit, so long as you have the rings."

"They're in the pocket of the garment bag."

"Well, then, I'm happy that she didn't burn your suit," Michelle said.

"Not that we know of," Molly added, and the three traded a concerned look.

"I don't know if you two staying together is the best idea. I can ask someone else to swap if this proves too difficult. I want you both to be able to enjoy the next couple of days, but I also don't want to ask the other guests who've already settled in to move," Molly said, chewing her lip.

"We'll be fine; neither of you has anything to worry about. I promise to be on my best behaviour, and if she wants me to leave, I will," he said, seeing the instant relief in their eyes. "All you two have to worry about is each other. I'll leave you both to your seating chart, and I'll show you the suits tonight before the party."

Walking towards the lift, August hoped Mia wouldn't be caught off guard again today by his arrival. The truth was, as selfish as it seemed, he finally had Mia back in some way, and he didn't want to let her go. At the very least, he now had an opportunity to apologise and keep her close, to remind her that they had been more than just his terrible decision to leave her without a word. He needed time to explain.

His mind immediately turned to the driver's comments about organising blind dates for Mia. He couldn't expect her to be single and longing for him, but the thought of another man touching her, or even being near her, made him want to scream.

"August!" Michelle called after him, and he stopped the lift doors from closing.

"Everything alright?"

"I don't hate you." She rolled her eyes, just like Mia did when she was frustrated. Even though they looked the same, they couldn't be more different in his eyes.

"Thank you?"

"I know you still love my sister, and I've never seen her as happy as she was when she was with you. I can't hate someone she loved and who made her so happy," Michelle said quietly, so the other guests in the lobby wouldn't overhear.

"I sense there's a but coming." He winced, not going to make excuses for himself.

"But don't make me regret not hating you. If you

upset her, then I won't be able to have you here, and that would break Molly's heart. So please don't make me break the hearts of two people I love most in this world."

"I love them too," he said, understanding where she was coming from. "I want to make things better, not worse. And if I can't do that, then I'll leave, before I even have to be asked."

"*Do* you still love her?" Michelle asked bluntly.

He hesitated, knowing he could lie to protect himself and his ego, but now wasn't the time for bullshit. "Yes, and I didn't leave because I didn't love her."

"Then why? Not even Molly would tell me, no matter how much I pried."

August let out a sigh. "I think Mia has the right to that answer first."

"Fair enough." Michelle nodded, stepping back, and he let the doors close.

"Mia?" August called out, opening the door to their room. The bathroom light was on, and judging by the steam escaping from under the door, she hadn't lost her love of baths, which meant she had her earphones in.

He didn't want her to be surprised when she got out, but stepping into the bathroom was out of the question. He could knock? Bloody hell, he didn't even know why he was second-guessing every thought. What if Michelle was right and she wasn't aware of who she'd agreed to share with? Surely she must have seen his name beside hers on the check-in list.

August dropped her bridesmaid dress on the antique poster bed and waited for her in the armchair by the desk after he unpacked his suitcase.

ia opened the dress bag hanging on the back of the bathroom door, expecting the steam to have helped relax the creases on her bridesmaid's dress. Instead, she found a black and navy tux inside.

Taking out her earbuds, she reached for her phone to call reception and ask if the bellhop had accidentally swapped her suit bag with someone else's. She had always wondered why hotels put phones in bathrooms; now she knew why.

"Mia?" August's voice through the door was unmistakable, and she put down the phone. "Sorry to disturb you, but I believe I've got something of yours."

"August? How did you get inside my room? You need to leave, right now!" she snapped, realising she must have grabbed August's bag when she'd practically leapt out of the sleigh. *So much for a relaxing bath,* she thought, wrapping the white fluffy towel tightly around herself and taking a deep breath. *Just give him the suit bag and he'll leave.*

"You mean our room?" he corrected, a hint of amusement in his tone.

She froze. *Our room? Only if hell freezes over.*

"You've got to be freaking kidding me. You're who I'm meant to be sharing the room with? You need to leave. I might be able to tolerate you being at my sister's wedding, but there is no way in hell I'm sharing a room with you for four days!"

"I thought you were okay with sharing," he countered, clearly confused. His calm composure only infuriated her, and she began pacing across the tiles. "The receptionist said you had agreed to the arrangement because of the snow."

She rested her forehead against the bathroom door. *Fuck!*

"Yes, I agreed to share, but I assumed the guest would be anyone but you," she argued, needing another bath to relax all over again. "Why didn't you refuse?"

"Because I thought you agreed, and since we were the last two guests to arrive for the wedding, there's literally nowhere else for me to go," he explained, far too calmly.

Not wanting to have this conversation through a door, she swung it open, not expecting to come face to face with him. Or more like chest to face.

"But I'll leave if you want me to. The last thing I want is to make you uncomfortable," August concluded, staring down at her, his eyes lingering on her towel.

Mia hesitated, recalling her conversation with Michelle. If she couldn't leave, neither could he. She moved past him, careful not to touch him.

"Great, so I make you leave, and then I'm the bad guy," she huffed.

"I'm not trying to make you look like the bad guy—"

"And like you said, where would you go? You're the best man – you can't avoid being here any less than I can." She didn't know why he looked so bashful; it wasn't like he hadn't seen her naked.

"There's only one bed..." His eyes darted to the large poster bed.

"You're sleeping on the couch."

"Happy to, and thank you. I appreciate you letting me stay, I know it's not easy—"

She cut him off. "We might be stuck together, but I don't need you to pity me. I'm not some broken-hearted damsel. And I don't have time to argue about rooming. I need to finish getting ready and downstairs before Michelle comes looking for me."

"Sorry, I didn't mean to sound condescending," he said, and she felt his eyes on her as she unpacked. "I just don't want things to be awkward between us."

She gritted her teeth, forcing out the pleasantries. "Why would it be awkward? You really don't have to apologise. I'm sure we'll survive a few days together." Why did his calm and apologetic demeanour piss her off so much?

"Sorry—"

"Say that again, I'll kick you out."

August zipped his lips, moving to pick up the dress bag

from the bed. "As pretty as the dress is, it's not my size, so I thought I should return it to you," he joked lamely.

Feeling his eyes on her back, Mia hung the lilac dress on her side of the wardrobe and zipped it up again. She couldn't risk anything happening to it. With her recent luck, she half expected it to burst into flames or catch on a nail.

"You don't want to wear it?" He frowned.

"I can't wear my bridesmaid dress to the bachelorette," she pointed out, wondering if he'd lost his senses over the past two years. He was right, though. It was pretty. Her sister had been kind enough to choose a dress that actually suited her bridesmaids, rather than selecting an unflattering style and shade to prevent them from outshining the brides.

"Right, my mistake." She could tell he was desperate to move the conversation away from their past and complicated present. "Can I have my suits? I need to show them to the brides so they can pick." He was hovering awkwardly by the bathroom door.

Mia took them off the bathroom door and handed them to him.

"Thank you."

His fingertips brushed hers, and her body cried out at his touch. Two years, and she still craved him. Suddenly, she wanted another glass of champagne to drown out her worst impulses.

"I need to finish getting ready. Can you turn around or find something to do?" she said, embarrassed by the pitch of her voice as she grabbed her little black dress and underwear from her bag. She wasn't going to get changed with him in the room. She felt vulnerable enough as it was.

"Don't mind me, I'll shower and give you some space."

And peace. "Perfect."

"Let me know if you need any help," he quipped, following her into the bathroom. She only grabbed her makeup from the marble sink and closed the door on him. With quick reflexes, he moved back before it hit him.

Leaning on the outside of the bathroom door, she took a deep breath, wishing it locked from the outside. Then again, she couldn't keep him locked up all weekend; Molly was bound to miss her best man.

I'm trapped in a living nightmare. I can't believe I'm actually sharing a hotel room with my ex at a romantic wedding. She pushed away from the door. *This is my hell, but I'm not going to let him see me sweat.*

AS SHE WAS FIDGETING with her long sleeves and securing her gold *M* pendant to show off the square neckline, Mia heard the shower turn off. Suddenly, she was the one feeling bashful. *Four days, it's only four days,* she repeated to herself, trying to stay calm. *We have the hen party tonight, wedding photos tomorrow morning, Saturday is the rehearsal dinner and I'll be busy decorating the cake, and then Sunday is the wedding. We'll barely have time to even notice each other.*

"Are you decent?" August asked, knocking lightly.

"I'm decent." *It's as good as it's going to get, anyway,* she thought, examining her hair freshly straightened, red lip perfected, and enough concealer to hide her lack of sleep. In the mirror, she watched August leave the bathroom with a towel around his waist. "Seems you're the indecent one. I could've passed you in some clothes."

"It's not like you haven't seen it all before." He removed a clean white shirt from his bag and laid it out on the bed. "You look beautiful," he added softly.

Mia ignored him and grabbed her heels so she could escape faster. She didn't want his compliments.

"Are we going to ignore each other for the next few days?" August asked, changing into his shirt. Her gaze traced the muscles on his back, recalling how it felt to drag her nails down his skin as she cried out his name.

She shook off the memory. *He left you, remember?!*

"I've nothing to say, and we need to be downstairs soon." She reached down to secure the clasp on her heels, but hesitated. Her nails were still wet. She didn't wear polish in the bakery, so this was her chance to have a pretty purple manicure.

"Let me help you," August said, kneeling in front of her. He was far too close, and the smell of his aftershave brought back *good* memories that she'd prefer to remain buried.

"I don't need any help," Mia argued, but before she could pull away, he lifted her foot onto his knee, his hand wrapped around her ankle, and she shivered. He wasn't allowed to help her, to make her *feel*.

"Don't be stubborn. If you let me help, then you'll be able to get away from me all the faster," he said, staring up at her. She smoothed down her short skirt so he couldn't see up it. "Being mad at me doesn't mean you have to ruin your nails."

He has a point. She resisted the urge to kick him away and run out of the room. Once August had fastened the second clasp, she felt like she could breathe again.

"The less we talk, the less we interact, the less likely we are to fight," she told him, tapping her foot, though he remained kneeling in front of her. "This week's important to our families. We need to smile and get along; the past is in the past. I've moved on. Can you?"

"I can do that," he promised. "I'm not going to do anything to spoil this week for Molly; she's like a sister to me, and I rarely get to see her. I know how important this is for both of them." The concern in his gaze made her hope he was truly genuine. "Maybe we can be friends?"

It felt like a dagger had pierced her heart.

"Friends. Right." Mia smiled through the pain and grabbed her clutch.

"I'm glad to have this back; the brides would've skinned me alive if I'd lost the rings," August said, letting out a long sigh. She watched him remove a red velvet ring box from his suit pocket and place it on the table by the flatscreen built into the wall.

Mia and Michelle trusted him with the rings? He must be closer to the couple than I realised. She wished her sister hadn't felt the need to lie to her – the secrecy hurt – but this was about their special day, and she couldn't blame them for wanting *everyone* they loved with them.

"Want to see?" he asked, holding out the box to her. "Molly made them to surprise Michelle. She's planning on opening her own jewellery store in Yule. She's been making rings and other pieces for Michelle all year, so she wouldn't be suspicious."

Mia opened the box. "They're gorgeous! Molly made this pendant necklace for me last Christmas, so I knew she was talented, but the engravings around the gold bands and the diamonds are so delicate. Michelle is going to love the sapphire in hers! I'm so pleased Molly's pursuing her dreams. I hadn't realised she was leaving the mine," she said, handing August back the rings to put in the small safe in the wardrobe.

"Now that they're getting married, I think she wants a safer role. I believe she only started in the mine to make her parents proud," he told her.

"My sister will love them." Mia stopped herself, realising how easy it was to talk to him. She didn't want to fall back into that habit. His uneasy smile told her he was thinking the same. She hadn't noticed he had got so close, and she backed away.

"You might want to remove that," she said, tapping the corner of her lip where his was pierced with a small ring.

"I thought you liked it." He smirked, sliding a black belt through his trousers.

She scoffed, wanting to erase those memories. "Molly asked for tasteful jewellery in photos."

"Right. My parents probably planted that idea in her head. Thank you for reminding me," August sighed. Mia hadn't met his parents; they usually stayed on the Outside, and he'd moved out before turning eighteen to live with the band. As far as she remembered, they'd never been particularly close. In the mirror, she found herself watching him remove the piercing. His hair was longer now, just past his ears, messy yet styled. Mia understood why he had been voted one of the top 30 sexiest men under 30 in GlaMore magazine last year.

Stop staring. He left you! she reminded herself again.

"Right. It's none of my business, anyway," she said.

"You are the maid of honour, so I suppose it's your duty to make sure everyone follows the rules," he mused.

Mia nodded. "Twin sister and all – it's my job to be at the bride's beck and call. I suppose she'll do the same for me one day. I already missed the engagement party, so I've some ground to make up." The thought of her own wedding made her uneasy; she'd once thought he would be the one waiting for her at the end of the aisle. As it turned out, he would be, just at someone else's wedding.

"Maybe it's for the best you weren't there," he said suddenly. "You should've seen your sister when she realised I was Molly's cousin; she was ready to kill, but Molly managed to talk her down. Not that I blame her – it was a shock for all of us. I didn't mean to ambush her that night, or you in the sleigh."

"Seems you have terrible timing when it comes to your arrivals… and departures," she said, trying not to stare as he buttoned up his shirt. Something she used to do for him.

"Ouch" – he winced – "but you've got a point. I can't seem to get it right when it comes to you."

"Maybe you should try harder." She bit her tongue, cursing herself. She hadn't meant it to sound like a challenge.

His eyes locked on hers, and her heart quickened. "You're right, and I plan to."

Mia stared at the carpet, unable to bear his eyes on her. "Regardless of your crashing the party, I wish I'd been there for them. But I was ill and didn't want to infect everyone else. Maybe if I had made it, this wouldn't be so awkward now."

"It seems fate wanted to bring us back together sooner or later. I hoped you'd be there," he added shyly.

"I would've thought you'd be too busy touring." Mia wasn't sure if she was pleased or annoyed that he'd wanted to see her. She'd been in Yule the entire time. If he truly wanted to see her, all he had to do was visit the bakery.

"I was, but I managed to slip away. I couldn't let Molly and Michelle down."

"And I could? I didn't decide to get sick," she snapped.

He smiled nervously. "No, that wasn't what I meant. I rarely get to see Molly from one end of the year to the next, so I didn't want to miss any part of the wedding."

God, his smile. She'd watched a few of his newer music videos when she couldn't resist thinking about him. They didn't do him justice, even in the sweatpants and over-sized hoodie he'd clearly travelled in. His smile nearly made her forgive the socks and sandals. Almost.

She rolled her eyes. "It's fine, I didn't mean to get so defensive." The air in the room was thick with tension, filled with all the things she wanted to say to him but couldn't. "I've got to get downstairs before the bride sends a search party."

She turned her back on him before she caved and begged him to tell her what had happened two years ago.

"Mia," August called after her, following.

"Yes?" She paused, her hand on the door handle. The way he said her name made her forget how much she was supposed to hate him.

"Your key?" he said, standing so close to her back she was afraid to turn around.

"Right." She glanced behind her and snatched it, then hurried out of the door before she broke completely.

After hours of playful bachelorette games, dancing until her feet hurt, and downing shots, cocktails, and champagne, Mia's mind was still haunted by thoughts of August, who was somewhere on the other side of the castle, probably having the night of his life. By the pink Christmas tree decorated with white and gold baubles, she snacked on a gingerbread replica of the castle in an attempt to soak up the last round of tequila shots.

The more I drink, the more sober I get, she mused, standing beneath the disco ball which cast shimmering reflections across the ornate ballroom walls.

"Mia, it's a travesty! We're out of champagne," Michelle shouted over the 90s classics from their childhood, tipping the last champagne bottle upside down and trying to extract every drop. Mia's twin looked every bit the happy bride in her short white sequinned dress and short veil, topped with a plastic silver tiara.

"Don't worry, I'll go down to the cellar," Mia chuckled. She had worked tables at the castle in school to earn some extra pocket money and knew where everything was. Besides, she was only taking the alcohol they'd ordered for the wedding. As the most sober person in the room, which was a low bar, she didn't trust anyone else to go to the wine cellar alone in the middle of the night.

"Want me to go with you?" Michelle asked, glancing at the other bridesmaids. They were on the small stage beneath the glittering disco ball, begging her to join them for a song.

"No, go have fun! They need a Baby Spice to complete the act," Mia urged, and watched as her sister drunkenly swayed over to get on stage. She doubted anyone else would notice her leaving; the room was buzzing with tipsy guests dancing to the bridesmaids' terrible karaoke. She didn't want to be a buzzkill, but she needed a break.

Mia reached the cellar door through the closed kitchens. The old door to the cellar was easy to open from the outside. She just had to be careful not to get locked in, as the lock on the inside had been broken for years, and no one had bothered to repair it. Mia propped the door open with a brick, just like she used to do when she worked here.

"Creepy, creepy, creepy," she muttered as she descended the worn wooden stairs to the musty cellar. Luckily, the lights were functioning, though the bulbs were few and far between in the spacious cellar filled with wine and whisky casks. The castle, one of the oldest buildings in Yule, had its own brewery.

Fortunately, the bar staff had kept the cases of beer,

wine, and champagne for the wedding party against the wall across from the stairs so that she wouldn't be taking from the castle's own supply. Filling a small empty crate with bottles of champagne, she heard some creaking behind her and hoped it was just the wood settling in the cold.

"Please don't be rats. Anything but rats," she muttered, only to scream when she saw a large shadow cast on the wine shelves.

"It's me, Mia." August grimaced, covering his ears.

"You gave me a freaking heart attack." Her hand flew to her chest. "What the hell are you doing down here?"

"The same thing you are! The bar was closed, so I got sent to do a beer run."

"Next time, say something! It's so spooky down here, I thought you were the ghost of Christmas past." She chuckled with relief, grateful she hadn't broken any bottles.

"I saw the lights on and figured you'd hear me coming down. I tripped over the brick by the door – nearly broke my neck."

"You moved the brick?" Mia demanded, whipping around to glare at him.

"I kicked it, to be precise, but don't worry – the brick isn't injured," he said sarcastically, as if she cared more for the brick than his neck.

"What a relief, but please tell me you didn't remove the brick from the door?"

He frowned. "I might have. Why?"

"Oh no, why!" Mia hurried up the stairs to find the door jammed. "Just when I thought this weekend couldn't get any worse." She stared down the stairs at him. "The brick was the only thing keeping us from getting trapped in here—"

Her scolding was interrupted by the lights going off.

"Didn't see that coming," August chuckled, far too calm for her liking.

"Fucking perfect," she groaned, resting her head in her hands. As if being trapped in the same hotel room with him wasn't bad enough. "At least the castle has generators, so the lights will come on soon." The only light keeping them from being submerged in complete darkness came from beneath the door and through the cracks in the old wood.

"We don't need to panic. Molly or Michelle will notice we're missing."

"Are you kidding? I don't know how your night's going, but everyone's too drunk on my side of the castle, and the heating doesn't work down here in the cellar. IT'S A CELLAR," she barked, turning from the door, only to come face to face with him. She hadn't heard him come up behind her.

She swallowed, pushing herself up against the cold brick; there wasn't much room for one person, let alone two, at the top of the stairs.

"Fair point." He tried to jiggle the handle, but the door didn't budge. Mia rolled her eyes – as if she hadn't already tried that.

Impatient, August shoved his shoulder into the door, but it would need a lot more force to be persuaded to free them. He tried again.

"As much as I don't want to freeze to death down here

with you, if you keep doing that, you're going to dislocate your shoulder."

"I've no intention of freezing to death either," he panted, rubbing his arm.

"Want to try kicking it down next?" she teased, enjoying his frustration. It was a nice break from her own.

"I would, but there isn't enough room. And as much as you would enjoy watching me make an arse of myself taking a tumble down the stairs, I'm not risking a broken leg," he countered, heading back down.

"Where are you going? There's no other way out."

"I'll sit here until someone comes and opens the door. You're very welcome to join me to keep warm." August sat against the floor-to-ceiling wine rack beside the crates set up for the partygoers. "Maybe they'll come looking when they realise their alcohol hasn't arrived."

"I'm fine," Mia lied, wrapping her arms around herself. Her lips were probably turning blue beneath the red lipstick.

"You're shivering, and that dress isn't going to do much to keep you warm."

"I wouldn't have to worry about keeping warm if you hadn't trapped us in here."

"I'm sorry I moved the brick, but it was a mistake."

"I'm getting tired of paying for your mistakes," she muttered to herself.

He frowned, watching her walk down the stairs. "What?"

"Nothing." She wasn't sure if he really hadn't heard or he just didn't want to argue.

"Maybe it's fate trying to bring us together," he suggested.

"And why would fate want that?"

"So we can talk." He took off his jacket and offered it to her.

"I've nothing to talk to you about." Mia stopped pacing and snatched it before her pride prevented her.

"Really? Nothing at all?"

She shook her head and slipped her arms into his jacket, even though it swallowed her. His scent was all over her, as if she was his all over again. Her heart fluttered like a giddy schoolgirl's, but her brain quickly dumped a bucket of cold water on her to snap her out of it.

"Alright, but could you please sit down? You're making me dizzy with all that pacing. You're just wasting your energy."

She didn't want to admit he was right, but she wasn't sure how long it would be before anyone came looking for them. Cautiously, she sat down beside him. His jacket served as a good buffer.

"You're shaking," he said. "Come closer."

"I don't need—" she started, but he quickly pulled her towards him, and a wonderful warmth travelled through her body. Avoiding his eyes, she stared at his chest as he placed his arm around her shoulder. Being so close to him was overwhelming. If she hadn't been shivering before, she was now.

"You can be stubborn once we get out of here," he said as she leaned back out of his grip, taking her fingers in a gentle embrace and warming them with his breath. She wanted to make some witty retort, but his proximity turned her to mush. His kindness felt almost cruel. "Do you have your phone?"

"No, I left it in my bag in the ballroom. You?"

"I think it's in my pocket."

"Why didn't you mention this before?" She slipped her hand into his jacket pocket and found it.

"I'm an idiot?" he chuckled. He wasn't wrong.

When the screen lit up, she stared down at… herself.

"Are you kidding?" She couldn't believe he still had their photos. She had deleted *most* of theirs, though she kept some in a folder she pretended didn't exist until she'd had too many glasses of white wine.

"What?" He grabbed the phone.

"The photo?"

"It's just someone sitting on the beach."

"Someone? That's me! You think I wouldn't recognise the bikini or my back? Your lockscreen is me!" It had been taken on the beach, not far from where August lived. She'd loved that beach, sitting with him on the sand and watching the sun go down. Mia found herself smiling, only for the memory to turn cold, triggering a deep ache in her chest.

"It's a picture of a painting by my friend Phoebe."

"Did she use my picture as a reference?!"

"I don't have any signal down here," August said, obviously trying to change the subject. But she wasn't having it. He'd agreed to share a room with her and had her photo as his screensaver – what the hell was he planning?

"We can agree to disagree," she said, starting to remove his jacket, but he rested his hand on her shoulder.

"Don't take it off," he sighed. "Phoebe saw the photo on my phone, and she wanted to use it as a reference for a new collection. She didn't know who the photo was of. I liked her painting, so I bought it to support her. I also didn't want anyone gawking at you on the wall of some gallery."

"Why would you care who gawks at me? *You* ended things." Mia breathed into her hands so he wouldn't be able to read her expression.

"Because I've never stopped caring about you." August took out his lighter. "Cup your hands around the flame; it'll help with the shivers."

A wave of heat surged up her arms, and it wasn't just because of the lighter. It had been a clever move, as it forced her to lean into him.

"Then why leave me back then?" She wasn't sure if it was the darkness, the champagne, or the numbing cold that gave her the courage to ask, but she regretted the question as soon as it left her lips.

"I'm sorry I broke my promise. I should never have left you."

"I don't want an apology."

"You need to listen—"

"No, I don't. All that matters is that you said you wouldn't leave, and you did. Where have you been to explain this? Why weren't you there when you said you would be? I loved you so much. It was agony to realise you were never coming back. You left without a word. You'd promised, and I believed you. I defended you for weeks, telling my sister and myself there must be a good reason. I fought my own mind because I needed to believe that." Once she'd started, Mia couldn't stop the floodgates from opening. "I don't need an apology. I need you to understand what you did to me – my heart. You didn't just break my heart, August; if you had, I could've picked it up and put it back together again. But you shattered it – my heart, my trust. I never knew love until you, but losing it nearly killed me. The hope that you would walk through the door and smile at me, that you would let me back in. I thought you were the one."

"I was. I am." His voice trembled, like he was trying to hold himself together as desperately as she was.

"That's worse, then, because you made a choice that wasn't about me! I need you to understand what your choice means. If anyone ever broke another promise to me, I think I'd go insane. I forgave you long ago for my own peace, because hating you only kept you close. Loving you without being with you was too painful, and I can't keep holding onto that. If you want to tell me why you left, I'll listen, but that doesn't mean we can ever go back to the way we were," she said, trying to keep her voice steady.

"I know it won't fix us, but I want you to understand why, because you deserve to know. I'm not expecting anything from you; I just need you to know I never wanted to leave you." August took a deep breath, then turned to look at Mia, who saw the heaviness of hurt in his eyes. "I'm guessing you know about the accident already."

Guilt and pain swept over her. She did know, but she hadn't wanted to bring it up, guessing how much it must have affected him, and she'd told herself it couldn't have had anything to do with him ghosting her.

"What you don't know is that things started to fall apart a long time before it happened. The morning I left you at the hotel, Cillian didn't attend the meeting. I went to his room and found him in the bathtub of his suite. He'd taken some pills, and whatever he had mixed them with had nearly killed him. I had to get him to the hospital."

Mia pressed a hand to her mouth. Although she had seen the lead singer of the band in passing, they had never actually met. All she'd known about him was that he and August were like brothers. There were only a few people August trusted, and Cillian was one of them.

"Cillian was spiralling. He'd always been a bit of a party guy, but he was getting out of control. I took him to the hospital and had his stomach pumped, and he told me he was going to go to rehab and get clean. I couldn't leave him. Nick and Axel wouldn't give me a chance to escape, and I couldn't tell them about you, about Yule. I was trapped."

"Why not call me, email, or something?" she couldn't help asking. "I would've understood."

He shook his head. "I know I should've, but I didn't want to bring you into my mess. I thought I could handle it, clean up his mess on my own. The four of us have always been family, and I was terrified of losing him, of everything falling apart. I know it was stupid not to reach out to you, to leave you in the dark. Everything just… felt like it was caving in on top of me. I felt like I was being torn in two, and I froze."

Mia tried to understand how he felt. Seeing Cillian so broken couldn't have been easy, but she wouldn't have to be trying to imagine it if he'd just let her in. "You should have given me the chance," she sniffled, wiping her nose with his sleeve, lying to herself it was the cold making her nose run. "I hate that you felt you couldn't tell me what was going on. I wish you had run towards me instead of away. I understand that you wanted to be there for your friends and keep me out of the mess, but you should have given me the chance to support you. I'd have told you that your mess is my mess, that's what being in a relationship means!"

"I wanted to see you. I wanted to talk to you, to tell you what was happening, but every time I picked up the phone, I just couldn't. The moment I heard your voice, I wouldn't have been able to stay away. I'd have chosen you over them."

"So, you stayed and decided to leave me in the dark. Thinking anything could've happened to you, thinking you just decided that you were done with me." Mia swung from anger to frustration. What she really wanted to be was held and told that their love had meant as much to him as it did to her. She couldn't believe that the person she wanted to comfort her was the man who caused her pain.

"I stayed. Our manager at the time had us on lockdown, so the news about Cillian didn't get out. He even begged us not to tell Phoebe, his girlfriend at the time. Nick's sister, do you remember?"

Mia nodded. Phoebe was a famous artist now.

"Cillian didn't want to worry her, so I thought once he

got out of rehab, I'd be able to come home and explain everything to you."

"But you didn't."

"Joke was on me. Turns out he never quit," he said, running his hands through his hair. "Worse, he was cheating on Phoebe. Cillian promised us he would tell Phoebe about the cheating and return to rehab, and I couldn't give up on him. I wish I'd come to Yule and told you what was happening, but I was trying to keep my band – my family – together, and I didn't know how to handle what he had become. His betrayal of her, of us. They've been my family since I left my parents, and I thought if I left, they'd fall apart."

Mia listened intently, dreading the conclusion to the tale.

"I thought everything was getting back on track. We were touring, and I was going to come back for Valentine's Day and beg for forgiveness... but then Phoebe caught Cillian cheating at our concert." August forced the words out like they choked him. "They got into a car accident, and he died on impact."

Mia didn't know what to say. She let him be silent for a moment, emotions churning in her chest.

"After being in hospital, Phoebe came to live with us. Between the grief of losing Cillian and Phoebe being blamed in the press, I wasn't in a place to be with anyone. I didn't want you to see me like that, as a shell of myself. I couldn't bring you home, not without explaining who you were, and I couldn't leave without explaining where I needed to go when they needed me."

"I thought you wanted nothing to do with me. We

were together for a year, and I thought it meant nothing to you." Mia shook her head. "I heard about the crash and panicked, but your grandmother told me you hadn't been in the car. It killed me not to reach out and check on you, but I thought that if you'd spoken to your grandparents and not me, it was just another confirmation that we were really done."

"That year with you meant everything to me, and I made a terrible decision. I was trapped, scared, and grieving. Seeing my best friend, a brother, betray the one person he loved most, and witnessing her distress, terrified me. What if one day we ended up like that, hating each other? I've never been good at expressing my feelings, but with you – you opened up my world. I left you before I could lose it. Then there was a crazy stalker after Phoebe, us, and I couldn't get you involved. I couldn't risk you getting hurt. I wasn't going to turn back up in your life only to hurt you again, to put you in danger. If I came back just as we were all being threatened, I wouldn't have been able to forgive myself."

"Did you catch the stalker? Are you still in danger?" she asked, her head swimming with all he'd confessed. "I just wish you had trusted me enough to confide in me what was happening instead of deciding what I could and couldn't handle."

"It's not that I didn't trust you, but I wanted you safe, and in Yule, no one could get to you. She's in prison, but it took over a year to get back to normal. We did a special tour in memory of Cillian, and Phoebe and Axel got together. Everything was starting to settle, and then Molly said she was getting married. I hadn't spoken to her in over a year... you weren't the only one I left. My grandparents only knew I was okay because they visited the Outside when they hadn't heard from me. They hadn't left Yule in decades, and by then I was too much of a coward to return and face you. So much time had passed; I had no right to come storming back into your life again. Then there was the engagement party, and running into your sister."

Settled into silence, Mia wrapped his jacket tighter around herself, wondering how she would've handled the situation he'd found himself in. If she hadn't been in Yule or had had her papers, it wouldn't have been a big deal for her to go to him, but the connection to Yule had put a bright red line between them, forcing them apart at the worst possible time.

"Are you going to say something? I don't think I left anything out, other than I'm sorry, and I hope you won't hate me for being so cruel," August said, his eyes searching hers for an answer.

"As much as I tried – and trust me, I did – I'd never hate you. I only hated what you did to us." Her confession was barely a whisper.

He pulled her in closer, and his presence untangled knots in her stomach. She forgot about the pain and betrayal. His tender grip engulfed her, and for a moment she let herself sink into his touch.

"But can you forgive me?" he asked, cupping her jaw and tracing her cheekbone with his thumb.

"I don't know. So much time has passed..."

She rested her hand gently on his chest to keep him away or pull him close, she wasn't sure, and she could feel his heart hammering. His eyes drifted to her lips, and her breath caught as she realised he was about to kiss her.

There was so much to process that she didn't know where to begin. Twenty-four hours ago, her biggest concern had been whether her gingerbread trees for the wedding cake had enough snap. Now, the man she thought had abandoned her was telling her that he'd never stopped caring for her.

Mia opened her mouth to speak, but the sound of the door opening startled them.

"Aren't you both looking rather cosy?"

They both snapped their attention to the top of the stairs, where Molly and Michelle were staring down at them.

"I told you they snuck off together," Molly attempted to whisper, but she was too drunk to be subtle.

"We didn't sneak off together!" Mia protested, stripping off August's jacket and dropping it on his lap.

"The door got stuck while we were down here," he explained.

"We were just getting more drinks for the party when the door closed, and the power went out." Mia stood up, wanting to create as much distance as possible between them.

She couldn't believe how close she had come to crossing the line. He was more intoxicating than the champagne, and she needed time to think. She still had questions, and she wasn't going to give in so easily. Even if she could get her head around all this information, she wasn't sure she could forgive him. Two years! If times got hard again, would he just leave her once more? She didn't know if she could forgive or trust him. Her heart begged her to wrap her arms around him and never let go, but her head reminded her of the earth-shattering pain when he'd left without a word. She needed to know that he would share things, both big and small, with her if she was even going to think about trusting him again.

Without looking back, Mia hurried up the stairs as if her feet were on fire, heading back to the ballroom, but Michelle followed closely behind, slowed down by the crate she carried.

"What the hell was that?" Michelle asked gleefully, taking a seat beside Mia at the table covered in lace-edged linen and offering her a glass of champagne. "You two were looking awfully cosy in the cellar. Sorry for interrupting. It all looked very tense."

"It was freezing down there; we had to huddle together to stay warm. Did you want to have two popsicles at your wedding?" Mia wasn't going to reveal all he'd told her – now wasn't the time or place. She also didn't know where to start.

"Sure, you were keeping warm." Michelle rolled her eyes. "But I think I'm going to have this picture framed." She shoved her phone in Mia's face, so close it was a struggle to focus on it. Mia took the phone, feeling a little nauseous at the image of her and August staring back at her. They did look quite cosy; if they hadn't been found when they were, she might have let him kiss her. *I can't believe my willpower is so weak. One day back in my life, and I ended up literally back in his arms.*

"Please delete that. Things aren't all right between us, but we've agreed to be civil since we're sharing a room— "

Michelle's glassy eyes widened. "You actually agreed? I was expecting you to kick him out!"

"He's staying on the couch," Mia clarified. "I couldn't kick out Molly's best man with nowhere else for him to go."

"Molly and I were so worried about you two sharing. We thought you'd claw each other's eyes out," Michelle fretted, twirling her flute between her fingers.

Mia chuckled. "I promise to wait until after the wedding photos are taken before clawing his eyes out. I don't want the photographer to have to photoshop in some eyeballs."

"Very funny, but did he tell you why he left?" Michelle grimaced.

"Do you really want to talk about this at your bachelorette?"

"Yes, I want to know everything. You've no idea how Molly and I have been dying for updates. Molly says he still loves you, and I want you to be happy." Her twin was clearly drunk and high on wedding fumes.

"Love was never our problem," Mia sighed. "Yes, he explained why he left. No, I don't want to discuss it, because I believe you owe me a dance. I didn't nearly freeze to death for champagne we aren't going to drink."

"Are you really okay?" Michelle asked, taking her hand – a moment of sense in her tipsy haze.

"Nothing dancing with my dear sister can't cure."

"A remedy I can truly support." Michelle jumped up excitedly. Together, they joined the dance floor with the other bridesmaids.

Early Friday morning, the alarm woke Mia. She opened her eyes, only to flinch when she realised her leg was between August's, her head on his shoulder, and his hand resting on his chest – his *bare* chest.

This is a nightmare.

Reaching over, she turned off her phone before it woke him. With a wince, she slowly moved her leg, then slipped her hand from his and tried to slide out of the bed as if she were a burglar sneaking away from the crime scene.

"Five more minutes, just let me hold you for five minutes," August begged, half-asleep, his warm body cocooned around hers.

Staring at the ceiling, Mia hesitated, not wanting him to let go. *How could I have let this man back into my bed? Did I give in at the first hurdle? One touch and everything is forgiven.*

"You were supposed to stay on the couch," she said. She'd forgotten how comforting it was to be held by him. Molly and Michelle had offered to let her stay on the couch in their suite, but she'd refused. There was no way she was going to let her Ghost of New Years Past ruin their happiness.

"When I got back, you were already asleep. It was freezing, and you refused to give up the extra blanket." He nuzzled into her neck, and she wished she had the willpower to shove him away.

"I've missed this," she admitted in a whisper, but luckily, he had already drifted back to sleep. They'd both got in so late, he was probably still drunk. Mia ran her fingers up and down his toned forearm. She wasn't sure when the five minutes he'd asked for ended, but she couldn't bear it another moment. Slipping out of bed, she escaped to the bathroom, desperate for a barrier between them.

Closing the door behind her, she shook out her limbs in frustration and grabbed a towel to silence her curses and cries of self-deprecation. All it had taken was one night for her to end up back in his arms. She glared at herself in the full-length mirror, scolding her body as if it were the guilty party, with a will and mind of its own.

He is bad for you, stop it, she repeated over and over as she brushed her teeth and showered, desperate to wash him off her skin. She didn't want his cologne haunting her all day. *He was half asleep and hungover; he won't remember what I said. Today is about wedding photos, Michelle, and Molly. What happened last night was a drunken lapse in judgment. If I'd been sober when he crawled in beside me, I would've kicked him out. Tonight, he's back on the floor or the couch.*

She slipped into her pink jogging set from the bachelorette gift bag Michelle had given her during last night's party to go downstairs for a quick breakfast, since they had to be ready early for the photos. She was desperately in need of some painkillers for her headache and porridge to calm her churning stomach.

SO MUCH SNOW had fallen overnight that even with the ploughs leading the way, it took twice the time it usually did to reach Mia's family's cabin by the lake. Most families in Yule had a small lake house, as many loved to skate or ice fish. Thankfully, the rush to get everyone out and organised for the wedding photos by Yule's frozen lake meant Mia didn't have to discuss last night's entanglement with anyone. She had barely processed August's confession in the cellar, let alone how she felt about waking up in his arms.

On their sleigh ride, much to her relief, August was far too busy nursing his hangover and having a quick nap to talk. She'd tried to get into another sleigh, but of course the maid of honour and best man had to travel together, so the photographer could get a shot of everyone in their sleighs before taking off. Mia had brought him some strong coffee and pastries from breakfast to rouse him and convince him to get in the shower. Her mum had warned her about being late when she'd arrived at the buffet to find her parents and the rest of the bridal party dressed and looking far fresher than she felt – a miracle, because they'd drunk a lot more than she had last night.

Molly and Michelle were already posed by the edge of the frozen lake, embracing under the starry sky. Molly wore an intricate, lacy, form-fitting gown, while Michelle's was long-sleeved and champagne satin. The moonlight was hitting the glassy lake behind them perfectly, and with the fresh snow on the trees, it looked every bit as magical as they'd hoped.

"Why did the brides have to change their minds about taking photos this morning? I feel like my brain is going to fall out of my ears," August groaned, offering his hand to help Mia out of the back of the sleigh. This time she accepted – she was in heels, and she couldn't risk slipping on the step or in the snow. Glancing around, she couldn't see anyone else from the wedding party, and she wondered if they were so late that the others had already come and gone.

"Because it's better to get the photos done now, before the next wave of snow. Or, worse, before the snow thaws into sludge and the lake floods," she said, noticing that he flexed his hand in his lap once she let go. Clearly, she wasn't the only one affected by their touches.

"Isn't it bad luck to see the brides in their dresses before the wedding?"

"Are you kidding? Michelle and Molly are far from superstitious. They bought their dresses together in Patty's Bridal Boutique. Even if she wanted to, Michelle can't keep a secret to save her life." Mia smiled. Her sister had always worn her love and excitement on both sleeves.

"Why am I not surprised?" August chuckled, watching

the couple. "They're so happy," he said, barely a whisper, like he was letting out a sigh. "I wish Molly's parents could be here to see her so happy."

"They can. I'm sure they're with her." The brides' expressions of love and certainty as they looked at each other made her heart tighten with joy and a hint of jealousy. She pulled the blanket she'd taken from the sleigh around her shoulders. "Between the frosty cellars, power outages, and snowstorms, remind me to get married in the summer."

"Noted." August winked playfully.

Mia rolled her eyes. The last thing she needed was to think about *their* wedding. Still, she wondered what a fresh start would be like, if trusting him again was even possible. Would she always be looking over her shoulder and wondering if he was going to disappear again?

"When I woke up and you were gone, I wasn't sure you'd be coming back. I didn't expect to wake up in bed. I'm sorry I broke the rules," August said quietly as the brides waved at them. He must not remember their morning snuggle.

"It's fine, we were both drunk." Mia brushed it off, not wanting to jog his memory. She waved back at the brides while the photographer moved them into another pose. "You got in later than I did, so I figured you needed a little more beauty sleep while I went to breakfast," she said, lifting the hem of her bridesmaid dress to prevent it from dragging in the snow as they walked down the path to the lake.

"Right, thank you for the coffee. My first thought was that you were avoiding me," he said, following closely behind like he was ready to catch her. "I thought I heard you say you missed me. Must have just been a dream."

Before she could admit that she *had* been avoiding him, not because she was angry about him climbing into their bed or couldn't forgive him but because she didn't trust herself around him, they were interrupted by her grandmother.

"Ducky! There you are. Why are you out here in the cold when we're all in the cabin keeping warm?" Grandma Ginny beamed brightly, her pink lipstick matching the flowers on her dress and furry white shawl. She was in her eighties, but she didn't look a day over sixty. "We were starting to think you wouldn't make it, but I see you were distracted." She gazed at August with admiration.

"Grandma Ginny, you should stay wrapped up in the cabin!" Mia hugged her to prevent further comments about August. Over Ginny's shoulder, she glimpsed August's smirk.

"Oh, hush. I've spent a small fortune to make sure no one mistakes me for anyone's grandmother, and I wouldn't want the groomsmen to hear you." Ginny winked, taking her granddaughter's arm. Despite how much she despised the title of Grandma, she loved her grandchildren. She huddled close to Mia so that August couldn't overhear. "I'd offer to leave you a groomsman, but it seems you've already caught the *best* man. I'm so glad they went with the black suits over the navy – far more classic."

Mia glanced at August, who concealed his chuckle with a cough. "I'm sure Grandpa wouldn't be too pleased to hear that." She knew how much the old couple loved each other, even if they also loved to drive each other crazy.

"I've got to keep him on his toes – keeps us young." Ginny winked.

"Have you met August?" Mia asked, not wanting to think about her grandparents' love life.

"We had the pleasure at the engagement party. Careful with this one, Mia, he's quite the charmer." Ginny nudged her playfully.

You've no idea. She sneaked a glance at August in time to see him blush.

"Can we get the maid of honour and the best man?" the photographer called out, waving them over.

"That would be us," Mia said, ushering August away before Ginny said anything else.

She didn't know about their past, and Mia wanted to keep it that way. She didn't want it to become wedding gossip. "So, you charmed my grandmother?" she asked, amused and confused by the thought of him making small talk at the engagement party.

"She did all the charming. I just sat there and listened," he said, pulling at his tie awkwardly. Mia smiled. Ginny loved anyone who let her prattle on uninterrupted.

"If you could stand by the bank beneath the trees, the lighting is perfect," the photographer directed them. "Can you get a bit closer to each other?"

Mia was relieved not to have to stand on the lake, even though it was frozen most of the year. The thought of it cracking beneath her feet terrified her. They moved around each other awkwardly, but the photographer shoved them together. Suddenly, it felt like they were posing for their own wedding photos.

"You didn't tell your family about us?" August asked, trying to stay balanced on the snow.

"We were going to, two years ago, but you didn't show up," she reminded him, keeping her smile bright. "If I had told my grandmother, everyone would know, and we don't want any attention taken away from my sister or Molly. You've never lived in Yule, but you should still know how much it loves gossip."

She side-stepped towards him, but the photographer shook his head.

"I know it's cold, but you both need to relax a little; you look like it's physically painful to get close," he called, reviewing the photos he had already taken. He tutted. "How about an arm around the waist?"

"Only Michelle knows about us?" August asked, doing as instructed. The gentle pressure of his hand on her lower back made her think he didn't want to make her uncomfortable, but the shadow of his presence only made her crave his touch all the more.

"And Molly. I wasn't going to brag about how my boyfriend left me. No one needed to know."

"Leaving you had nothing to do with wanting to avoid you or meeting your family. You've no idea how much I wanted to come back to you," he said, his tone verging on pleading. Mia wanted to comfort him, to forgive, but she couldn't drop her guard. After all, he had come back for the wedding, not for her.

"Much better," the photographer said as August held her closer. The smell of his cologne was dizzying, and his hand on her waist sent a shiver up her back. *Why does my dress have to be backless?* Mia forced a smile, trying to focus on the camera and get away from him as fast as possible. August cleared his throat and pulled at his navy tie once again. No matter how much he fidgeted, he was only making it more crooked.

"Here, lean down, and I'll fix it," Mia offered, and he did as he was told.

"You're not going to strangle me, are you?" August smirked down at her as she loosened it.

"Not until after the photos are taken," she teased, slapping his lapels before turning her attention back to the photographer who was still snapping away.

"That buys me some time to ask about whether you thought about what I told you last night?" he muttered through a false smile, so the photographer didn't scold them again.

"Can we not do this now? The more we talk, the longer this is going to take," Mia said, shaking out her foot as she slipped into a pile of snow. Her toes were already turning blue.

"Later then, but I need you to know that I still love you. I want to start again, for us to date. I want to make up for all the lost time even though I know I can never actually make up for it. I'll spend the rest of my life apologising for what I did to you, but I want to prove that I'm in it for keeps now. I'm yours, then and now." August's words cut through her as his eyes lingered on hers.

"That's perfect! I've got everything I need. If I wasn't mistaken, I'd think you were the two getting married. The chemistry between you is a photographer's dream."

He loves me. He's mine. Does he truly mean it? Mia wanted the snow to swallow her whole, and August pulled at his tie again.

"We need a few group shots, and then we can all get out of the cold," the photographer announced, breaking the tension. Mia spotted her sister and Molly looking far too amused behind the cameraman, who was gesturing for Mia and August to come closer.

If they weren't wearing their bridal gowns, I'd be pelting them with snowballs, she thought. Not needing to be told twice, she stepped out of August's embrace. His hand slipped from her waist as the rest of the wedding party was summoned to join them.

"What if I promised you next Christmas? What if we could start over with our plans?" he asked, staring down at her.

She wanted to believe him, to trust him, but she couldn't face that same heartbreak again. The desire to protect her heart was too close to outweighing her yearning for him.

"I don't want promises. I want to see your love in your actions, not in your words," she said softly. Despite her words, she felt her body leaning into him, betraying her better judgment.

August's smile faded. Before he could respond, the photographer swiftly separated the families and friends, sparing her further discomfort.

"Everything okay?" Michelle asked, standing beside her for their family shot.

"Never better," Mia assured her, smiling happily despite her heart breaking.

August

After brunch in the castle, August drank enough espresso at the bar to keep him awake for the rest of the year. Instead of curing his hangover, it only heightened his anxiety. He kept reliving his conversation with Mia by the lake. He'd hoped to speak with her on the sleigh ride back to the castle, but she had ridden back with her parents, leaving him to her grandmother. Ginny had promised to try to set them up after the wedding, but she obviously didn't realise quite how much he was trying to win Mia's good favour.

The photographer's callout of their undeniable chemistry in front of their family had been agonising. He was trying to win Mia over, not scare her away. If the lake hadn't been frozen, August would have drowned the man for making her pull away from him – but not without saving the camera first. He wouldn't want to lose Molly and Michelle's photos in the name of revenge.

Mia appeared carefree, warming up with the bridal

party and her parents at the bar. August took a deep breath as his eyes wandered over her slinky dress, which hugged her curves and accentuated her slim waist. The fabric was tied at the neck, concealing her cleavage but revealing glittery highlights on her shoulders, making her look even more tempting.

"Do you want to save some coffee for the rest of us?" Molly asked, sitting down on the barstool beside him. She'd changed out of her wedding gown into a dark green wide-leg suit with thick silver jewellery she'd made herself.

"Not particularly. At least it's not Irish." The bottles at the back of the bar looked increasingly tempting. Still, it was far too early in the day for hard liquor.

"Thank you for saving the vodka for a more responsible hour," she teased. "Things are going that well with Mia, huh?"

"I wouldn't say awful, but I wouldn't say well."

"You did ghost her after a year of dating."

"Can you please stop reminding me? I'm well aware of what happened and that it was a dick move on my part. I wish I could take it back, but I can't. So now I'm prepared to grovel for the rest of my life if it means convincing her to trust me again," he said, fighting the urge to cross the room, lift Mia over his shoulder, and drag her back to their room. *It's the 21st century, not the Stone Age.* But that didn't stop him from longing to undo the satin bow of her halter top and kiss the sensitive spot between her neck and collarbone, recalling how it used to make her gasp.

As if she'd sensed his thoughts – the lustful ones – her gaze locked on to him from across the room. He watched her chest rise and fall, wondering if her flushed cheeks were from the fire beside her or something more. Fuck, he needed a drink.

"You really can't hide the fact that you still love her," Molly said, watching Mia leave the room. He figured she was going to get changed now that she had warmed up.

"Loving her wasn't the problem. If I didn't love her so much, I wouldn't have left. You know what happened with Cillian and Phoebe; I freaked out, and then he died, which fucked up all our lives. I couldn't escape that, which was the perfect excuse for me to freak out and leave the only person in this world who makes me feel like I can breathe."

"Have you told her that?"

"I told her last night."

"When she was a captive in the cold cellar, with no way out?" Molly asked.

"Bad idea?"

"Not as bad as leaving her, but better not to hold your audience captive."

"I can't get any part of this right." He sighed. "Don't you have a bride to attend to? Shouldn't you be focused on being in love and less on my love life?"

Molly shook her head. "Not going to get rid of me that easily. You got rattled by life, and you bolted. You lost a friend who betrayed someone you loved. You're human; we all mess up. On my first date with Michelle, my anxiety was so bad that I had a panic attack in the middle of a restaurant. I thought I'd never see her again, but people love us not just in spite of our faults, but because of them. If you truly want her, you'll have to earn back her trust, which will take more than just a weekend. Make her see that you're not just here for the wedding, but that you came back for her."

"You're comparing a panic attack on the first date to me leaving her on New Year's after a year?" August chuckled, loving Molly all the more for trying to ease his guilt.

"Okay, so it's not the same. However, things go wrong in every relationship, and all we can do is move forward. You clearly want to move forward with her, so apologise - but *properly*. Really acknowledge what you did wrong and see if she feels the same. If not, then I'm sorry, but you'll have to move on."

"I don't want to move on," August said, spinning the coffee saucer on the bar.

"Well, you can sit here, or you can get off your butt and fight for her."

"I get it. I'm not giving up. I'm serious about repairing our relationship, but I don't want to be harassing her; I want to give her time to breathe."

"Room to breathe? You're sharing a room! Things can't be so terrible if she didn't kick you out yet. Besides, she's had two years of space, and this weekend isn't going to last forever, even if the weather is determined to snow us in."

"I've the storm to thank for that. If it wasn't for the snow, I'm sure she would've insisted on staying at home."

"Even the weather wants you to end up together," Molly teased, eating the cherry out of her cocktail. There was no reasonable time for drinks for the bride. It was her time to indulge.

"Shouldn't you be getting back to your bride?"

"I can take a hint, but I wanted to thank you for coming. I know it's not easy to get away, and with Mia it's a whole other level of complicated, but it means the world to me that you're here. You're like the big brother I never wanted." Molly winked, resting her hand on his forearm. August wasn't a fan of physical touch, but she was one of the few exceptions. Without her forcing hugs on him when they were kids, he doubted he ever would've got over the hurdle.

"And you're like the little pain-in-the-arse sister I never wanted."

"Speaking of being a pain in the arse," she said quietly, "I do have an alternative motive for coming over while Michelle is distracted with her family. Do you think the snow will affect the garden plan for New Year's Eve?"

"Don't worry, I've made sure the gardens are set up perfectly. The manager promised they've covered everything we need, and they've hired extra staff to keep the area clean of the worst of the snow. It's been a good excuse to keep the area closed so Michelle won't find out by accident," he promised. "Don't worry, everything is going to be perfect."

"Thank you. I'm so anxious about singing, but I'd do anything to make Michelle happy, and with you on stage with me, I think I can pull it off."

"You'll be great! I'll be right by your side, so even if you make a fool of yourself, you won't be alone," he teased, and she punched his shoulder. She was strong as hell from years of mine-work.

"Thank you for giving me the nudge I needed. I never

would've been able to get my butt on stage without your help. And thank Nick for helping me with the vocal lessons. I would've loved to have the whole group for the wedding. Maybe one day Yule will be more lenient about friends learning about us."

"I already told him it was just a small wedding. He loved the watch you made for him, and he was happy to help." He didn't want her to feel bad. She and Michelle had discussed having a wedding on the Outside and a bigger wedding in Yule. Unfortunately, it had proved to be too expensive; with Molly buying and setting up her jewellery shop, they didn't want to spend too much.

"In case you need a little nudge, Mia's in the kitchen checking on our wedding cake, by the way," Molly said as she left.

She was right; this weekend wasn't going to last forever. August left the busy bar in search of Mia. The central kitchen was busy prepping for lunch, and the chef told him Mia was using the private kitchen through the breakfast room.

August found her alone, leaning over individual cake tiers, scraping off the white and pale pink marbled icing and grumbling to herself about something. Gone was the bridesmaid dress, replaced with black leggings, pink legwarmers, and an oversized knitted jumper with the sleeves rolled up. Her hair messily gathered in a clip on top of her head, she looked just as beautiful – even more so, lost in her passion.

"Everything alright?" August asked, wondering why she was undoing her hard work.

He thought she would tell him to leave her alone to

work, but instead she glanced up at him with relief in her eyes. "Thank God, I thought you were Michelle or Molly. I can't let them know about the cakes."

"What happened to them?" They still looked good.

"The kitchen staff checked on the fridges after the power outage, and someone took the cakes out of the freezer and left them out on the counter by accident," Mia told him, wiping her brow with her forearm. "The icing separated, and now it's just a buttery mess. It's my fault for not checking on them this morning, but with the late night and leaving early for the photos, it completely slipped my mind."

"They melted? I didn't know cakes could melt," he said, realising the marble effect wasn't intentional. "And it's not your fault – you weren't the one who left them out."

"Doesn't matter now who's to blame. Buttercream left out in the heat of a kitchen? It didn't stand a chance." She sighed. "Luckily, I brought some spare icing in case anything went wrong, but I need to finish getting all this off, redo the crumb coat, and let it chill before the brides find out."

"Can I—?"

She rounded on him before he could finish. "I appreciate you wanting to make things right between us, but right now I don't have time to talk. I've got to get these cakes iced and chilled before I can start decorating, which will already take me a couple of hours."

"I just wanted to see if you needed any help." Like Molly had said, she'd been a captive audience in the cellar; he wasn't going to force her to talk if she wasn't ready.

Mia hesitated, seeing right through him as she always could.

"I used to love watching you work when we were together. There must be something I can do," he offered. He'd spend hours just watching her in silence. Her passion and creativity was easy to fall in love with.

"If I let you stay, will you promise not to distract me and let me work?" she asked sternly.

"Is it really so hard to be around me?" He'd hoped they had made some progress in the past twenty-four hours, but every step forward felt like they were going two steps back.

"Yes! Of course it is," she exclaimed, setting down a spatula covered in icing. "You make me forget how to breathe, how to think. If we hadn't been trapped together in the cellar, I would have remembered to check on the cakes after the power went out. Instead, all I was thinking about was you and what you told me and how desperately I want to forgive you, but I'm terrified that you'll hurt me again, and I don't have time to be distracted this weekend!" She pressed her lips together hard, and her eyes widened as if she couldn't believe what she had just said.

August moved to stand behind her and heard her gasp as he rested his hands gently on her hips so she couldn't run away. He turned her around to face him.

"What if I can't stay away from you either?" he asked, pressing her up against the counter. "What if I don't want to? What if I can't stand to spend another day thinking about you but not being able to touch you, talk to you?"

Her breath caught at his words, encouraging him. *To hell with the repercussions. Touching isn't breaking any rules.*

Her skin flushed when his knuckles grazed her cheek. A sigh escaped her lips, tempting him to kiss her, to see how she would react, to find out if she was just as incapable of avoiding him as he was her.

Uncertainty coursed through him – the same adrenaline rush he felt before heading out to face a stadium full of fans, but her rejection meant so much more. He didn't know if he would be able to survive it. He was teetering dangerously close to giving in to his desires, yet he was trying to give her the space she needed to accept that he was truly there for her.

Neither said a word as he ran his thumb over her full, soft lips while his eyes met hers. His heart clenched painfully, noting a flicker of vulnerability in her eyes and the furrow of her brows. He tilted his head, bringing him dangerously close to her lips, and a mischievous grin spread across her face as she traced gentle fingers down his chest, instantly warming every inch of him. His body ached with anticipation and longing at the thought of kissing her.

Mia closed her eyes, and August surrendered to the magnetic pull between them. He rested his hands on the counter behind her, his nose brushing hers. He wanted to give her every millisecond to back out, but she leaned into his embrace. She was as desperate as he was. But as he leaned forward, he realised his hand was on the chopping board, not the counter, and they stumbled as the board flipped and knocked them both off balance.

"No! No! No," Mia cried as the cake tiers crumpled to the floor. Sinking to the floor before him, she picked up handfuls of the ruined cake tiers. He couldn't believe what he'd just done; the horror on her face felt like it would imprint on his memory. How many hours of work had he just ruined in a matter of seconds?

"I'm so sorry, Mia. It was an accident. I thought I was leaning against the counter until I felt it tip. I'm so sorry, we can fix this," he said frantically, wiping the cake on his chest before kneeling to clean up the mess. The only small mercy was that he'd changed out of his wedding tux and into a jumper and jeans, or the brides would have killed him twice – once for the cake, and then for the tux.

Mia's laugh cut off his panic as he helped her gather up the mess of cake and icing, only for her to slap it back on the tiles, confusing him. Maybe she had started drinking early.

"Are you okay?" August asked, crouching down beside her – stupid question, really. He scraped the ruined tiers back onto the chopping board and tossed the mess in the bin to give her a moment to breathe.

"No, I'm not okay. I'm meant to be decorating the cake at this stage, not starting again." Mia's laughter turned into a groan as she straightened up and brushed the icing from her hands. "Now I have to start from scratch with very little time. Why did you have to come in? Do you enjoy turning my life into a mess?"

"I'm really sorry. This is the last thing I wanted to happen. I got caught up in the moment," he said softly, mortified by the disaster he'd caused. "I can help you fix it – let me help you. I'll do whatever you need. I can ask if the hotel can spare some extra hands to help you get the cakes redone. I'll cover any costs; tell me what you need, and I'll get it done."

She let out a long sigh. "Are you kidding? We can't tell anyone about this. What if it gets back to the brides that they don't have a wedding cake anymore?"

August winced; she was right. The fewer people who knew about his major fuck-up, the better for Molly and Michelle's sake.

"Can you grab some paper towels and help me?" she asked, picking at the icing smudged into the white tiles. "We've got to clean this up before my sister or anyone else comes in. Michelle will freak out if she learns the cake is ruined. I'll have to get the cakes done again today, and worry about decorating tomorrow before the rehearsal dinner if I'm going to get it finished." She looked like she was going to cry.

"Can we do the baking here? They should have what you need, right?" he asked, hoping she wouldn't have to travel into the village in the heavy snow.

She shook her head. "I've got everything I need back at my bakery; it'll be faster if I'm in my own space and know where everything is."

"Do you have your bell?" August asked, recalling the small magical gold bell she used to use to come and visit him on the Outside while they were dating. "That way we don't have to worry about getting caught in the snow, and spending time travelling to and from."

"We?" She frowned.

"It's my fault for distracting you. I want to help."

"Arguing with you is only going to waste time, so, fine. But I don't have my bell. I've already wrapped it up and given it to Michelle and Molly so they can use it to travel anywhere in the world for their honeymoon."

August knew there was usually only one family bell per generation, and since Mia had lived in Yule the longest, she'd had it until now. "That's a great present," he said, slopping more cake into the bin.

"I know, but it doesn't help us now. Do you have a bell?"

"No, but I've got an idea," he said, picking up the kitchen phone and ringing the front desk. "Can I talk to Martin, the night manager? I know he isn't working yet, wake him up! If you could connect me to his room, I'd greatly appreciate it."

"The night manager?" Mia whispered, but he pressed a finger to his lips.

"Sorry to disturb you, Martin. I've a favour to ask."

"Colour me intrigued, but if this has anything to do with the gardens on New Year's Eve, I've already done everything I can to make sure the snow doesn't affect your plans," Martin said gruffly, clearly having just woken up.

"And I really appreciate it, but I've another favour I need you to help me keep quiet."

"What can I do for you?"

"I need to borrow a sleigh for the day. I can't risk relying on the taxis with the snow warning, and I need to be able to get back into the village and out on my own time," August explained.

The line went quiet.

"I don't know," Martin hesitated. "What if you get stuck in the village? We'll be a sleigh down for the northern lights viewing tonight."

Maybe a bribe would help. "I wouldn't ask if it wasn't an emergency. I'll owe you one."

"Okay," Martin caved. "I'll call down to the stables and have one prepared and pulled round to the front steps in fifteen minutes."

August couldn't hide his triumphant grin. Mia clapped her hands silently as she listened in.

"Tickets to your next show?" Martin went on. "My daughter was devastated; she couldn't get any for your last tour."

"No problem, and I'll throw in some backstage passes to sweeten the deal." Helping her get to the bakery safely and fixing the mess he'd created was the least he could do for her.

"I'll win Father of the Year award," Martin exclaimed. "Let me know if there's anything else you need!"

"Any luck?" Mia asked when August put the phone down.

"Martin's going to let us borrow a sleigh to take into the village for the day, but we've got to be back before the guests leave for the late-night rides to see the Northern Lights," he said, hoping that would be enough time.

Mia let out a low sigh of relief and wrapped her arms around his neck. The sudden assault nearly knocked him off balance, but she didn't seem to notice as she clung to him, thanking him over and over again. August wrapped his arms around her waist, steadying them both. They settled into a comfortable silence; he didn't know what to say, he just didn't want the moment to end.

"S-sorry," she stammered eventually, struggling out of

his grasp. "Thank you for helping. There was no way I was going to be able to walk back, and I couldn't have asked Michelle for our family bell back without explaining why."

"I'm the one who caused the mess – I should help you fix it."

"I should have just enough time to get it done. I forgot about the lights being on the wedding itinerary. I know Molly and Michelle wanted to get a nap in before dinner, so that should buy us a few hours."

"And with an extra set of hands, we'll be there and back before anyone even knows we're gone," he agreed.

Her smile faded. "You don't mean you're coming with me?"

"I'm not letting you go alone. The laneways are tricky, and there's a snow warning in effect. You'll need some muscle in case you get stuck in the snow," he reasoned.

"I can drive a sleigh in any weather – this isn't my first storm."

"Many hands make light work, and if I don't ensure you get there safely, your sister and my cousin will kill me. Consider it part of my apology. Also, you'll need someone to hold the cakes on the way back." August wasn't going to give in; he'd go with her, or she wouldn't go at all.

Her eyes narrowed as she considered his point.

"You win, but we should get going. I want to be back before it starts to get dark and we can't see the ice on the roads," she said, her confidence waning.

"Couldn't have said it better myself." August gestured for her to lead the way out of the kitchen. She rolled her eyes, and he eagerly followed her to the foyer.

Just when they thought they were in the clear, Michelle caught them by the front door.

"Mia? August? Where are you going?"

"Just have to run a small errand. Back soon. I'll get the sleigh ready," Mia said quickly, disappearing. August tried to follow, but Michelle grabbed his arm.

"The sleigh? Why are both of you leaving? There's still a snow warning in effect," she reminded him, staring at him intensely.

"We've got to go out for a little bit, but we'll be back soon." August didn't have the time or desire to explain about the ruined cake; Mia was waiting outside in the cold. "Please, Michelle, we wouldn't go if we didn't have to."

"Don't hurt my sister again; there are plenty of places in Yule to hide a body," Michelle warned quietly, tapping him on the chest. August believed her, and he didn't want the brides to worry that they weren't coming back. *She'd definitely bury me six feet under if she knew I destroyed her wedding cake, trying to flirt with her sister.* He kept the thought to himself.

"Trust me, I'll make sure to get Mia back to you safely. The sooner we go, the sooner we'll be back," he promised, realising he not only had to win back Mia's trust, but that of the people who cared for her. Michelle was Mia's twin; if she was against him, he didn't stand a chance.

"Don't make me regret this," Michelle said, finally giving in and releasing his arm.

"You won't. Otherwise, I'll bring back a shovel and dig my own grave," he said, hurrying out the castle doors as Mia pulled up in the sleigh.

After a brisk sleigh ride through the streets back to the heart of the village, Mia and August pulled up outside her bakery. The exterior lights on the shopfront radiated a cosy glow against the snow-covered road, with its gold-painted sign, Sweet Pastries, promising comfort and a delicious treat inside. In a village where night never set, some lighting was required for safety. Mia slowed the reindeer to a stop so that August could hop down and help guide her down the side of the shop, where the sleigh and reindeer would be safe while they were busy inside.

As soon as they entered, the aroma of sugar and butter filled the air, wrapping them in a cosy familiarity. The scent of her home away from home instantly soothed Mia, but she didn't have time to linger. Unlocking the door, she immediately headed to the kitchen, where shelves stocked with jars of spices, bags of flour, and colourful extracts greeted her like a safety blanket. To

Mia, these ingredients were more valuable than jewels or dresses; her kitchen was her true home.

August switched on the lights while she started grabbing the ingredients for the cakes. She was surprised he remembered where the switches were. Perhaps he truly meant that he hadn't forgotten her or their time together.

"Okay, let's start again," she sighed, gathering all the ingredients she needed. Thankfully, she had enough fresh raspberries and freeze-dried raspberry powder for the mini heart-shaped meringues and white chocolate floral decorations. Lying everything out on the table, she noticed August rolling up his sleeves.

"Put me to work! Consider me your humble servant," he said eagerly, putting on one of her pink aprons covered in gingerbread men.

"Have you baked at all in the last two years?" Mia asked, trying not to smirk at how cute he looked in his apron. She had shown him a few tricks while they were together.

"I helped my housemate Phoebe make cupcakes for her boyfriend for Valentine's Day," he said, quite proud of himself.

Adorable. Still, she eyed him warily.

"I ruined the other cakes, so let me help," August said at her hesitation.

She didn't think it was a good idea to have a novice help with so little time, but it probably would also speed up the process. She was relieved he didn't bring up what had occurred just before the cakes had toppled to the floor; there wasn't time to talk about the almost kiss.

"If you're sure, but I'll talk you through each step," she

warned. Grabbing her black apron from the wall, she handed him her notebook with all the precise measurements they needed. The priority was getting the cakes in the oven and out to cool.

"Grab the bowl from the stand mixer and cream the butter and sugar together until pale and fluffy. Then add the eggs a little at a time, beating as you go until they're fully incorporated," she explained, once he'd measured out the right ingredients. She chewed her lip to stop herself from smiling at the crease in his brow as he combined the milk, vanilla paste, and vanilla extract, then added them to the creamed mixture.

"Sift the flour in?" he guessed, and she nodded.

Once the dry ingredients were incorporated, she let him divide the mix between the six Christmas-tree-shaped cake tins, each smaller than the last, to make the perfect tiered cake. As stressful as it was having to redo the cakes, she had to admit it was nice baking with him – better than lounging around the castle and obsessing over his confession before heading out that evening to see the lights.

"Now I need you to measure out the ingredients for the meringues and chocolate flowers, while I whip up the gingerbread," Mia instructed, securing her hair up in a claw clip. She could never focus with her hair down.

While the cakes baked in one oven and the miniature gingerbread men in the other, Mia prepared some fresh raspberry and vanilla buttercream, leaving the meringues to August. They worked around each other with such ease that she felt as if no time had passed at all between them; it stung just as much as it comforted her.

"I think this is ready," August said, and she went to check the meringue to make sure the egg whites and sugar had formed stiff, glossy peaks.

"Perfect – just fold in the raspberry powder." She handed him a small dish with the exact amount needed. August added the dehydrated raspberry powder with exaggerated care, as if he was afraid it would explode instead of just turning the mixture a pastel shade of pink. What was this man doing to her heart? He was like one of those dogs that looked intimidating but had the biggest heart.

"Done." He smiled broadly, only to frown when he caught her staring at him. "Did I do something wrong?'

"No." She shook her head. "You're doing great. Just grab me the piping bag fitted with the small circular tip from the other counter." Time to remove the vanilla cake tiers from the oven and set them aside to cool on a wire rack before trimming them to size. At least the vanilla sheet cakes for the rest of the guests had survived, and should be safely in the fridge back at the castle.

"Are you sure you trust me to pipe the meringue hearts?" August asked, using a spatula to scrape the mixture into the piping bag.

"I trust you; you've a steady hand," Mia said, gathering another piping bag. "And I need to make mini white circles for meringue snowmen, so we'll save some time if we're both piping."

"Gingerbread figures, snowmen and raspberry hearts – I can't wait to see how it all comes together," he said, piping the hearts with extra care.

"I know it seems like a lot, but trust the vision. Once

I've piped the trees on the edges and added the figures, then the snowmen and hearts are tastefully placed, it'll be the perfect Christmas wedding cake," Mia said, determined to give her sister exactly what she'd asked for. "Careful not to squeeze too hard when you start to run out—" Before she could finish, the metal piping tip popped, tearing the piping bag and smearing the mixture all over his hands.

"Damn it." August grimaced, putting down the ruined bag and wiping his hands with a tea towel. "Why am I such a fucking clutz around you?" he muttered, and she tried not to laugh at his embarrassment.

"Your hands are probably getting tired. I can finish the final tray, if you want to start washing the dishes, and then we can get out of here quicker," Mia said, filling another bag with meringue. Luckily, there was plenty of extra mixture.

"I got it. I'll be more gentle." He smirked.

"That wasn't really your style," she muttered under her breath. She couldn't believe she'd just said that. She wasn't supposed to be flirting with him, but she couldn't help it; he was too damn tempting. *Why did he have to come with me? He's making it impossible to hate him!*

"I can be whatever you want me to be."

"Focus," Mia said, cursing herself for the slip of the tongue. "Let me show you," she added, handing the piping bag to him and moving to the other side of the table to rest her hands over his. "You've got the shape right – just relax the tension in your hands; that way you'll have more control and your hands won't get so tired. You want to place the tip gently on the paper and then lift as you squeeze."

She demonstrated, feeling his breath on her ear as he leaned over her to see what she was doing better. They did a couple together, and she glanced over her shoulder to find him watching her instead of their hands. She put down the icing bag as a shiver crept up her spine. He was too close, and she couldn't focus.

"I think you can manage the rest," she said, removing her hands from his. She put the tray they had finished into the oven and took out another lined tray, but before she could turn around and put it on the counter, August wrapped his arms around her waist, his hands flat on her tummy. Her stomach tightened as her breath caught.

"You promised you wouldn't distract me." Her words were breathy as he rested his chin on her shoulder.

"Not the first promise I've broken," he said, his lips brushing her ear, making her swallow her own desires.

"Really? That's the line you want to go with?" Mia tried to make it a joke to break the tension, but his hands slipped down to her hips and turned her around. She could see a hint of green around the iris of his eyes. He tilted his head closer to hers, and her heart quickened as she thought he was about to kiss her. She closed her eyes, but when his touch disappeared, she found him smirking at her.

"You've some meringue on your cheek," he said, swiping his thumb across her cheekbone as her cheeks flared hot. He released her, and she giggled through her mistake, trying to recover from her embarrassment. Clearly, he was winding her up on purpose.

"Let me know if you need more," she said, tossing the ruined piping bag into the bin and placing the metal tip in the sink. However, when she turned around, she didn't have a moment to think before his lips met hers. His hands on her waist pulled her firmly against him.

"I needed more," he rasped, resting his forehead against her. She froze in his arms, torn between her desire to kiss him and the want to protect her heart, but she felt her resolve dissolve as his nose brushed hers.

"I meant more meringue mixture," she said, wrapping her arms around his neck and pulling him down. *One kiss won't kill me.*

"We really need to work on our communication." He chuckled, but her teeth sank into his lip, blood pooling before being stolen by her tongue. He hissed, pulling back.

"Punishment for breaking another promise." She smirked.

His gaze darkened. He reclaimed her mouth, and a coursing fire ripped through her every limb. His large hand covered her breast and squeezed, making her gasp, before he reached out to clench the edge of the table, leaving not an inch between them. The empty tray clattered to the floor.

Mia scratched at his back, shuddering with every teasing kiss along her jaw and neck. His face settled between her shoulder and neck as he lifted her up onto the counter. Her thin leggings allowed her to feel every inch of him pressed against her. His body hadn't forgotten her either.

At least this time the cakes were safely on the other side of the room, so there was nothing to ruin. Her legs tightened around his hips, and he growled his pleasure at her body's desperate response to his. Breathing ragged, he lifted his head to fuse their lips. Mia's mind whirled. Two years she had waited to feel this again. Her heartbeat thundered. Her fingers left his skin and slipped into his hair, both tugging him away to catch her breath and pulling him closer because she could never get enough. He smiled against her lips, and she knew her body was telling him everything he had longed to hear. Her mind might not have forgiven him, but her body was a traitor, and loyal to his every touch and tease. All she could do was brace herself while he kissed her. Hard, hungry, and relentlessly exploring. It was as if all that was unspoken between them was pouring into each other with every kiss and caress.

The timer on the oven cut through the passion, and Mia found herself reaching for him when he eased her legs from around his waist and moved away. She touched her swollen lips, trying to gather her senses. August stared at her intently, his breathing rough, as though waiting for her to scold him or break like a china doll.

"I'll take the meringues out of the oven, if you want to finish the final tray," she said quickly, moving off the counter before she could say anything about what just happened. Her body was still humming and begging for more, but the timer had spared her from giving in to her primal instincts.

"Right, I'll get to it," August said, picking up the fallen tray and getting to work, though not without sneaking glances at her over his shoulder. He looked as nervous and flustered as she felt.

"The meringues are perfect," she beamed, as the mini hearts came out of the oven – a welcome distraction from his perfect lips. *I should've known better than to let him come and help; of course he was going to be a giant, six-foot distraction,* she thought, noting that the cakes were cooling nicely.

"Great, we might actually make it back to the castle before Martin comes looking for his sleigh," August said, finishing up the hearts.

"Here's hoping," she said, starting to tidy up.

Once the cakes had chilled, Mia began applying the crumb coat while August started washing the dishes. He used to do that for her when he visited her after work. By the time he'd finished, Mia had carefully packed the cake tiers, icing, gingerbread, and meringues into some catering crates, making sure they were secure before loading them onto the sleigh. With all the decorating and stacking planned for tomorrow, she wouldn't have time to finish the details as neatly as she'd initially intended, but at least she *had* a cake. Focusing on it was the only thing preventing her from obsessing over August's hands on her body and how she was losing the strength to resist him. Spending time with him in the kitchen felt too much like the comfort of the past, and she felt her heart start to thaw towards him.

They finished locking up the bakery as it approached nine o'clock. They'd be a little late with the sleigh, but it was earlier than she'd expected, thanks to August's help with the cleanup. If he hadn't been with her, she wouldn't have made it back before midnight.

August

August held the cake tiers so tightly on the journey back to the castle that he was afraid he would crush them. He was so focused on protecting the precious cargo that he didn't utter a word.

It helped that Mia wouldn't look at him since they'd left the bakery. He didn't know whether it was because she regretted what had happened on the counter or if she wanted more. He was hoping for the former, even if his approach hadn't gone exactly to plan. He'd meant for her to come to him, to go at her pace, but one look from her and he'd lost the battle.

He licked his lips, sore and a little swollen from where she'd bitten him. He'd let her bite every inch of him if it meant she'd let him get close again. When he'd held her close and felt her lean into him, he'd realised he wasn't the only one aching for them to be close, and when she'd kissed him back, he had lost all sense of control. Two years was an eternity, too long to be apart from her. He'd never go that long without her again.

Luckily, the road to the castle had been freshly ploughed so that they could park the sleigh right at the front door, next to the others ready for the trip up the mountain pass to see the northern lights. The other wedding guests were too busy preparing to leave to pay them much attention and to August's relief, there was no sign of the brides.

"I should get the cake and put it in the fridge before we're noticed," Mia said, taking the crate from his lap.

"I can take it, it's heavy," August said, hopping out of the sleigh after her.

"Don't worry, I'm stronger than I look." She smiled softly, looking at the guests getting into the row of sleighs. "Besides, you should go with the others if you want to see the lights. You aren't in Yule often, so this might be your last chance for a while."

August didn't know if she was just being thoughtful or if she wanted some space. The last thing he wanted was for the wall between them to be reinforced just when she was starting to let him in.

"To be honest, I'm wrecked and hungry. How about some room service once you're done getting the cake and all the trimmings safe and secure?" he asked, hoping she would want to spend the night with him instead of heading up the mountain.

"You don't think we'll be missed?" Mia asked, holding the carefully wrapped cake in her hands as they walked through the foyer.

"I doubt it." August shrugged. He was afraid that

asking her outright might scare her away. "They'll be too busy staring at the stars and trying not to freeze their arses off."

"I'll meet you back at the room then?" she asked, pausing before she disappeared through the kitchen doors.

"Absolutely." He clenched his jaw to stop himself from smiling like an idiot.

Heading down the corridor, he ran into Molly outside their room, wrapped up in enough layers that all he could see were her fingers and eyes.

"I was looking for you and Mia! You've both been MIA all day. Are you ready to go? You might want to wear a few more layers for the lights – you aren't as used to the weather as we are."

"Mia and I aren't going to make it in time for the lights; we've been out all day, and Mia has been so stressed that she hasn't taken a break to eat," August explained.

"Oh no, we'll miss you both." Molly's frown deepened. "Michelle told me you and Mia had plans, but why would she be so stressed that she wouldn't want to eat? When I told you to make peace, I didn't mean to stress her out."

August cursed himself for letting that slip. "I didn't stress her out, and everything's fine. There was a slight cake emergency that's now sorted. We even managed to spend a few hours together without a single argument." He would have preferred to spend the day with her without accidentally ruining her hard work, but he did feel slightly smug that it had gone so well under the circumstances.

"The cake? What happened to the cake?"

Molly panicking was the exact opposite of what he wanted, considering all the effort they had gone through to make sure she didn't find out. "Nothing – we just had to go to the bakery to pick up some extra bits, so Mia can start putting it all together tomorrow. It's all safe and tucked away in the kitchen fridge. I can't do anything about the snow, but I'll make sure nothing else spoils your big day."

Molly sighed, allowing August to breathe again.

"Okay, I trust you. It's not a big deal if you can't come tonight, but please make sure not to stress Mia out any further. Our precious cake is in her talented hands, and you're already a distraction," she said, slapping him on the shoulder.

If only she knew how successful my distractions were. He kept the thought to himself. He knew Molly would be happy for them, but he didn't need the brides running to her and asking her questions. Baby steps were crucial if he was going to win back Mia's heart.

"Have a good night under the stars. Mia and I will hold down the fort." He winked.

Molly rolled her eyes before hurrying down the hall as Michelle called to her from inside the lift. "You too, and try not to burn the place down."

In their room, where August was safe from the risk of saying something wrong again, he added more logs to the fire and took off his coat and wet shoes. The staff had already turned down the room and lit the fire. He couldn't believe he'd almost told Molly about the cake. He let out a sigh of relief and rubbed his hands over the fire, cold from the journey back. It was incredible how much the temperature dropped as the hour grew later in Yule.

About to close the curtains to keep in the heat, he noticed the space heaters and fairy lights on the balcony. *It might be a lovely way to end the day, with food and a magical view,* he thought. He dialled down to the front desk.

"Hi, I was wondering about ordering some dinner. Is room service still available?"

"Yes, we've got a twenty-four-hour service. What can I get for you?" the woman said, and he could hear her typing away.

"Great," he said, picking up the menu from the bedside table. "Can I get the gluten-free tomato pasta with extra chicken and roasted veg?" he said, recalling her favourite order. Mia had always had a sensitive stomach and avoided gluten where she could – a challenging task for a baker who spent her life surrounded by it. "Can I also get the chocolate cheesecake with the raspberry sauce instead of the ice cream?"

"Absolutely."

"Thanks, and I'll get an order of medium rare steak and fries, but could I get an extra serving of fries and ketchup?" Mia would steal his, and her obsession with ketchup meant an extra serving wouldn't go to waste.

"Another dessert?"

"The lemon sorbet, please," he requested, in case the cheesecake was too sweet for her.

"Your food should be at your room within the next forty minutes, and the charge will be added to your room bill."

"Could you make sure all the charges for the room are

charged to the card ending in 0418?" It was the least he could do, after everything.

"I'll make a note for reception, and they'll update the bill," she said politely. He thanked her for her help before hanging up. Now he just had to set the scene. After she'd worked so hard to fix the ruined tiers, he wanted her to be able to relax.

Out on the balcony, he cleaned the snow off the glass table and turned on the space heaters behind the lounger. While they were heating up he removed the covering from the lounger, relieved to find it dry, before heading back inside just in time to hear the bathroom door opening.

"Sorry, I didn't hear you come in," he said quickly, turning to close the door and pull the curtains closed to avoid ruining the surprise, only to get a surprise of his own when he found Mia standing in her underwear behind him. His heart threatened to stop. "Or that you were changing," he stammered, turning his back to her to give her some privacy.

"What were you doing out there?" she asked, like it was nothing. He heard her walking towards him and froze when her hands slid over the back of his shoulders and down his back.

"Just getting some air while I was waiting for the food to arrive." August fought to get the words out, unable to think about anything other than her hands or what she was doing. He didn't know what had got into her, but he sure as hell wasn't going to question it.

"Are you going to look at me?" Mia asked softly. "It's not like you haven't seen it all before." She rested her forehead against his back, her hands slipping slowly, tentatively, around his waist, until they rested lightly over his abs. His gaze dipped down to where her fingers sat just above his belt buckle. He was afraid to move in case she let go; he didn't want to scare her away, but the warmth of her body against his had him fisting his hands by his sides to remain in control.

"I'm sorry," he said, low and gravelly. He wasn't sure what he was apologising for – maybe for his desire to turn around, sweep her up in his arms and toss her on the bed, and do all the ungodly things he'd thought and dreamed about for the past two years. Slowly, he reached back, his fingers brushing her hip to make sure she was real. He heard her breath quicken.

"About ogling me? What if I said I like you looking at me?" Mia pulled on his belt, forcing him to turn and face her.

"Mia, are you okay? Did something happen downstairs?" His eyes met her heated gaze.

"I'm just finishing what you started in the bakery," she smirked, rising to her tiptoes; then they were kissing, skin to skin, hands caressing.

Hunger and desire took over, and August walked her backwards to the bed, lifting her onto the edge of the mattress. He ran his hands up her thighs. Her fingers clawed at the sheets in search of something to ground herself; he loved the effect he had on her, but it was nothing compared to what she did to him.

She had got his jumper and T-shirt off and was reaching for his belt when a knock on the door ruined the fun. The lust left Mia's eyes, and panic took its place.

August groaned as she covered herself with the blanket and hopped off the bed.

"I'm going to shower – you should get the food," she said quickly, running away as though he had burned her.

August buried his face in the pillow, letting out a string of frustrated curses, before he gathered his senses and let out a long sigh to calm down. He wanted to murder the person on the other side of the door, even if they were doing their job. Right now, all he was hungry for was Mia.

Once he heard the shower start, he opened the door and let in the trolley of food, even tipping the grinning waiter instead of strangling him for ruining such a perfect moment.

When Mia emerged from the bathroom, steam trailed behind her. She was wearing the band T-shirt he had left in their room after his shower, beneath an open fluffy robe. Cute, cosy, sexy – she was trying to kill him. He'd never thought he could be jealous of fabric.

"Looks good on you," he said, smiling at how the white robe swamped her. "If you want something warmer, you can have my sweatpants?" he added nervously.

"Thank you. I enjoy feeling like the abominable snowman in your giant clothes." She took the sweats from him. August swallowed, diverting his gaze from where the T-shirt landed at the top of her thighs as she pulled on his sweatpants. He'd missed her freckles, and suddenly wanted to make sure they were all right where he had left them beneath his new favourite T-shirt.

"I've missed seeing you in my clothes," he murmured, closing the gap between them. He noticed her close her eyes as if waiting for him to kiss her again. Instead, he knelt and rolled up the bottoms of the grey sweatpants so she wouldn't trip.

Her eyes snapped open as she realised what was happening. "How kind."

"My pleasure." He smiled at her blush. She placed a finger beneath his chin, tilting it up, then pressed her lips against his, but he stood up and stepped away before he lost his nerve.

A flash of hurt settled in her eyes. "What's wrong?"

"Don't think I don't desperately want to finish what we started, but this weekend isn't just a wedding fling for me. I want you – all of you. You don't have to say anything, I know you need time, but I need you to know that I'm in this for the long haul. For as long as you'll have me, I'm yours," he said, taking her hand and brushing her fingertips against his lips. The spark was undeniable.

She sighed, nodding as if she was arguing with herself as much as he was. "You're right, we should take this slowly. Where's the food?" she asked, fidgeting with her sleeves. "You didn't eat it all while I was showering, did you?"

"Put on your slippers and follow me." He winked, leading her out onto the balcony. The further they moved away from the bed, the better.

"This is—" Mia stammered, staring wide-eyed at the candlelit meal, the lounger covered in blankets and cushions creating the perfect cosy nest. "Very romantic."

"Too much?" He winced, hoping he hadn't overdone it. Mia looked like she didn't know whether to run or sit down. He prayed for the latter. He had two years of grand gestures to catch up on. "I wanted to do something special for you. I promise it's just dinner." He removed the metal lids from the plates, hoping the smell of the food would convince her to join him.

"Is that chocolate cheesecake?" She beamed, eyeing the desserts.

"Your favourite."

"You're using food to buy back my affection?"

"Is it working?" He smirked, ushering her towards the lounger and wrapping the blanket around her shoulders before climbing in beside her.

"Maybe, but you know dessert is my weak spot. I'm starving, and you can relax – I'm not going to bolt," she added, sitting cross-legged and reaching for the cheese-cake. "Thank you for ordering all this. I'm surprised you still remembered what I like."

"I haven't forgotten a thing about you," he told her, biting into his perfectly juicy steak. Still, he hesitated at the edge of the lounger. Watching her stare up at him in his clothes, her lengthy hair lying loose and wavy over her shoulders, she looked so beautiful that he didn't trust himself. "Can I ask why Michelle loves New Year's so much? I've never been to a wedding with both Christmas *and* New Year's in the theme before."

"Molly's favourite holiday is Christmas, and Michelle's is New Year's Eve. So they decided to combine the two," she said, snatching a few fries from his plate even though there was a spare portion right in front of her. *Some habits die hard.* He smiled to himself, loving how she hadn't changed. "Our parents would make a big fuss about New Year's when we were growing up. Like most families in

Yule, Christmas is absolute chaos. Since our parents volunteered in world-mapping for the festive season, ensuring every house receives its fair share of dust, they were exhausted on Christmas Day. So, New Year's became our special time together. Michelle and Dad would go hiking up the mountain and watch the northern lights. Mum and I would cook. Then we'd exchange presents and watch the fireworks at midnight. They always made it feel like we were about to undertake some grand adventure in the new year."

"I see. Getting married at the castle at Christmas has always been Molly's dream, which is why I was so terrified about messing it up for her," he said, finishing his steak.

"When we were together, you didn't really talk about the Yule side of your family," Mia said. "I don't even remember you mentioning Molly, and yet she treats you like a brother."

"I rarely come to Yule, except for the holidays. Before I met you, I hadn't been back for a few years because I was so busy with the band taking off. It's never truly felt like home to me. Sure, my parents lived here, but they left to go to college, so I didn't grow up here. The band is part of my daily life, my home, and my family."

"Makes sense. I feel the same about the Outside; it feels so vast and empty. You were the only part of it I loved. Even though we were together for a year, when I think back, it felt so fleeting – but maybe that's because I didn't think it would end," she confessed.

Loved. Past tense. The thought made him put down his fork.

"I do have some great memories here; it was always like a secretive, magical adventure coming to see my grandparents," he said, trying to keep the conversation positive. "Molly was always by my side, and she was the only one I could bear to be around when we visited. She didn't make me feel like a freak, because I hated talking to people, and I couldn't stand the loud noises or crowds. I repaid the favour when her parents died. I didn't treat her with kid gloves or pity her. She picked the castle because of her parents – they visited it every Christmas."

Mia nodded. "Makes sense why she was adamant about it. They were only able to get this booking because of a cancellation; otherwise, she and Michelle were willing to wait four years."

"You know how the castle staff love to decorate with the fairytale of Yule, celebrating the village's history? They'd have afternoon tea and dress up. Since her parents worked in the mine, they rarely got dressed up or had time off; harvesting dust never stops. But they tend to get some reprieve in December, since the dust requirements have been met, all going to plan. Molly always got a new dress for the special day. Having the wedding at the castle probably makes her feel like they're part of her day."

"I never knew that. Molly doesn't talk about her parents much."

"It's hard for her to talk about them; she rarely even talks about them with me," he admitted, knowing he was guilty of the same trait. "I'm the same, I tend the avoid the difficult topics. As you know."

"Michelle is like that, but I've always been the opposite. I need to talk things out or I feel like I'm going crazy.

Probably why you and Molly get on so well, because you process things the same way – probably why she fell in love with Michelle. Michelle and I tend to fight about everything, but we always manage to resolve it quickly. The last thing we fought about was—" Mia stopped mid-sentence and wiped her lips with her napkin.

"Me?"

"Sorry, I didn't mean…" She cut herself off again. "I can see how hard you're trying to make this better."

"Don't be sorry, I've some ground to cover with your family. I wouldn't blame them for hating me." His curiosity got the better of him. "Can I ask what the fight was about?"

"Michelle told me that it was a good thing you were gone, since we'd have to break up eventually, so it was better to do it sooner rather than later. It wasn't about you as a person, but how we live our lives. If we'd been caught, we weren't only risking ourselves but Yule's existence. Michelle was probably right; I didn't have my guardianship papers, and we were being naive. She had just started seeing Molly at the time and was stupidly happy, which made me jealous, so her advice was very much unwanted. I argued that she didn't know what it was like to want to risk everything for the person you loved."

"But we were making it work! We were going to go to the council, get your papers. It wasn't like we were going to hide forever," he reasoned, surprised by Michelle's take, since she had been supportive of him trying to win Mia back.

"But we didn't get that far." She shrugged. "I think she

believed you chickened out at the last minute. Going to Yule's council and having our relationship stamped for approval is tantamount to engagement, and maybe you weren't ready. It's easy to disappear from my life when I technically don't exist in your world."

"I didn't chicken out, and you exist in all my worlds. My world doesn't make sense without you in it," August said, cupping her face so she was forced to look at him. He could see her eyes filling with tears before she gently removed his hand and went back to her food. He wasn't sure if she believed him.

"Let's just enjoy our dinner and forget the past," she said with a forced smile. "I'm glad we skipped tonight's outing for a more private viewing. It's nice to have a bit of reprieve from the other guests; I didn't expect everyone to keep asking about my love life and when it's going to be my turn. I suppose it's part and parcel of being the maid of honour. Small town, endless whispers. I can't count how many times customers have tried to set me up with dates for the wedding..." Mia trailed off as if she had revealed too much.

"I'm sure having me around is cramping your style and keeping you away from all your potential suitors." He didn't want to know about her dating life, but he couldn't expect her to have waited around for him for two years.

"Terrible, isn't it?" she teased, but she placed some of her blanket on his lap. "But I've got to admit having a certain rockstar around hasn't been all that terrible. Certainly been a distraction." She smiled at him.

"A good distraction?"

"I'm not sure yet; the jury is still out on you."

"Trust me, I'm guilty as hell of wanting to keep other men away from you, but I know I've no right to be possessive of you after what I've done. You've every right to find someone else after what I did. If I could go back and do it again, I would do everything differently." He wished he could read her mind, or let her into his own, so she could see how much he loved and had missed her.

"Are you going to finish your dessert?" she asked, changing the subject.

"You can have it. The sorbet's a bit too bitter for me, and with all the food I've eaten the past couple of days, I don't think my fans will appreciate what's happening to my abs." He patted his flat stomach, sure he couldn't manage another bite. Hours on stage and touring kept him in shape.

"No one would kick you out of bed over a few extra pounds. You look better with some stuffing," she muttered through a mouthful of sorbet.

He stared at her, waiting for her to realise what she said, then chuckled as she hid under the blanket.

"I've missed us," he said, pulling at the corner of the blanket to reveal those gorgeous green eyes and taking her hand as she sat up a little.

"Me too." She confessed, and he held her hand tighter to his chest.

"Your heart is beating really fast." Her eyes widened.

"Has been since I first met you," he confessed.

"You can't say things like that."

"Why not?"

"Because you make it impossible for me not to love you."

Mia took her hand back and pulled the thick blanket up under her chin, but she didn't move away from him. Did that mean she still loved him? Could he dare to hope that part of her heart was still his?

"Then my plan is working," he said, pressing his lips to her hair.

"Stop trying to use your charms on me, and watch the lights," Mia instructed, still cuddled into him.

He didn't dare say another word in fear of breaking the perfect moment. He'd never thought she would let him hold her again, let alone spend the night in the same room with him under the northern lights. If he blinked, he worried he'd wake up back in his house with his bandmates, and find the past few days had been nothing but a dream.

His hand gently brushed against her thigh, making her instinctively inch closer to him, drawn by an unspoken connection. Her hand slipped into his, and she rested her head on his shoulder as the lights appeared in the sky above the mountains. They watched in silence, wrapped up in each other.

He wasn't sure how long they were out there, or when Mia fell asleep. Gently, he carried her back inside to bed, wanting to protect her from the cold. He hesitated, intending to be a true gentleman and take the couch, but as he moved to leave, she softly grasped his wrist, anchoring him to her. Carefully, August lay down beside her, and she, seeking comfort, slipped her leg between his and rested her head over his heartbeat, just like she used to.

Mia did a little happy dance as she finished placing the final gingerbread house, iced with tiny windows and a snow-covered roof, on the cake. The village and forest scene had even surpassed her original plan. Admiring her eight hours of labour, she couldn't wait for the brides to see it.

Carefully, she lifted the completed cake and put it in the fridge. She took off her headphones, tidied the kitchen, and then left to get ready for the rehearsal dinner. She hadn't had a chance to think about her evening with August last night, how close she'd come to nearly giving in to her desires. As much as she wanted to be with him, she'd cursed the arrival of the food for interrupting them. But when she'd woken up in his arms, it had felt like a blessing in disguise, because it meant they'd spent the whole night communicating instead of letting their bodies do the talking. Physical intimacy had never been their problem, and now she knew he meant it when he said he didn't just want this to be a fling. If they wanted to start again, they needed to talk things through and learn to trust each other once more.

Instead of dreading his appearance, she found herself watching, waiting for him to appear through the kitchen doors. But Michelle and Mia had obviously been keeping him busy with preparations for the rehearsal dinner. They only reunited when it was time to get ready for dinner. He looked as exhausted as she felt.

"Can you help me?" Mia asked, stepping out of the bathroom in her dark green satin midi dress. "The zip is stuck on the lining."

He sat on the edge of the bed, and she lifted her hair while his fingers worked at freeing the snagged zip.

"Can you pass me…"

Before she even finished asking, he handed her the black strappy heels. Her feet were already sore from decorating all day, but she couldn't wear her trainers to the rehearsal dinner.

"Thank you, and…"

She turned around, and he winked at her, holding up her teardrop pearl earrings.

"You read my mind," she said, putting them in.

"Beautiful," he said, standing at her back in the mirror to tuck a few loose strands of hair into her low bun. His fingers grazed her shoulders, sending shivers down her arms. She wished her body didn't make her reactions to him so obvious.

"Stop teasing and get dressed," she ordered. They didn't have time to fool around.

An urgent knocking came at the door. "August! Open the door!" It was Molly's voice. "We've got an emergency!"

"What's wrong?" August asked, opening the door.

Molly rushed in, only to stop and stare at Mia. "I'm sorry for interrupting..." She looked at his state of undress, and then back to Mia. "Mia, hi, I thought you were already downstairs with Michelle."

"We were running late because I was busy finishing up the cake," Mia said, hoping no one was hurt. "Is everything okay? Has something happened to Michelle?"

"No, she's fine. I didn't mean to frighten you, but I need to talk to August."

"If you're having cold feet, I'm sure if you talk to Michelle—" Mia started, wondering if was the pressure of the whole weekend getting to her.

"No, it's nothing like that."

"You might as well tell her, because she's only going to keep guessing," August said.

"Tell me what?" It felt like her stomach dropped. *What is he hiding from me now?*

"I'm meant to be singing tomorrow, before midnight, as a surprise for Michelle," Molly told her, and Mia let out a sigh of relief.

"I guessed August might do something, but I didn't think you sang! I'm sure Michelle is going to love it," she beamed. "Don't worry, I won't tell Michelle a thing."

"Sorry we kept this a secret from you," August said, putting his arm around her shoulder. "Molly wanted it to be a surprise, and she didn't want too many people to know in case she backed out."

"In case I chickened out," Molly clarified, "but it

doesn't even matter now because the band we hired is sick, so they can't make it for the reception. I can't get up there all on my own, and what are we going to do for the New Year's party? We can't have a reception without music!"

"I'll perform with you so that you won't be alone on stage. We can do an acoustic version of the song," August said. "As for the band... hmm. It's not like I can call my own."

"I might be able to solve your band problem," Mia said eagerly. "Kevin Klaus's girlfriend is in a band, and they performed at the Christmas Gala last year. I think they'd love a chance to perform."

"Really?" Molly squealed. "I remember them, they were good, but would they be free so last minute?"

"I'll ping them and let you know after dinner," Mia said, picking up her phone and already texting Kevin. He had been a loyal customer because she allowed him to work on his laptop in the bakery all day. Hopefully he'd be able to get back to her soon so Molly could enjoy her rehearsal dinner. "Let's not tell Michelle until we know for sure whether or not they can perform."

"I won't say a word. She's worked so hard to make everything perfect, I don't want her to be stressed tonight," Molly said.

"Just worry about having a good night, and leave the rest to us," August ordered, guiding Molly towards the door. "Now get back downstairs to your bride before she wonders where we all are and senses something's wrong."

"Good point. I'll let you finish getting ready." Molly let out a sigh of relief as August opened the door for her.

"Thank you both for helping. I don't know what I'd do without you."

"Don't mention it. We're here to serve," Mia said, giving her a reassuring hug before she left.

"Thank you for reaching out to your friend – you saved the day," August said. "I'm pretty useless here."

"You're not useless. I'm sure having you on stage with her will make the experience all the less daunting and all the more special," Mia assured him as he finished buttoning his shirt and securing his cufflinks before they headed down to dinner together.

As the best man, Mia had expected August to be sitting beside Molly, but she suspected there had been some switching of the place cards when he sat down in the seat next to her.

"You messed with the seating arrangement, didn't you?" she accused him as the winter vegetable soup was served. The smell was the very embodiment of Christmas in a cup.

"I'd never," he scoffed, refilling her water glass.

"Liar."

"I may have bribed your sister with show tickets for her and her friends to let me sit beside you," he confessed, resting his hand on her thigh beneath the table.

Mia moved his hand back to his own lap, worried

Michelle, on her other side, would notice. She wasn't ready for others to ask questions. "Then I suggest that you enjoy your dinner and keep your hands to yourself."

"Your wish is my command." He leaned in close, and she tried to concentrate on her soup.

"Eat up before it gets cold," she ordered, not allowing him to tempt her, even if the mere sight of him made her hungrier for more than the delicious dinner. It was served promptly – the Yule staple of Christmas dinner, turkey and ham with all the trimmings, followed by mince pies and custard. Mia would happily live on stuffing and cranberry sauce, especially with mince pies for dessert, forever. August slid one of his mince pies onto her plate, and she beamed, happy he still remembered how much she loved them.

Her phone buzzed in her clutch once dessert was cleared, and everyone started to get up and move about the room. Kevin told her that the band would be happy to help with the reception, and all it would cost was a round of free pastries and coffee. She was delighted to oblige.

"Good news?" August asked.

"Kevin said the band can help! They'll come by tomorrow during dinner and set up," she grinned, and August wrapped his arms around her, squeezing her tightly. She froze when she noticed Michelle staring at her over his shoulder. She eased out of his embrace, and August got up to speak to Molly by the ice sculpture. From Molly's happy squealing and how she wrapped her arms around August, Mia knew she had got the good news. *Crisis averted.*

"What was that all about?" Michelle whispered.

"The snow warning has been lifted – I just got an alert from the local business group," Mia lied, though the message had actually come through earlier. It was the only cover she could think of on the spot.

"Oh, I must've forgotten to tell Molly. The manager told me earlier about the update. I didn't realise she was so worried."

"You know her – she wants to make sure tomorrow goes perfectly," Mia said, feeling bad about lying to her sister, but it was for her own benefit.

"Speaking of going perfectly, that was some hug August gave you. Has sharing a room helped thaw your relationship?" Michelle teased, as their empty plates were cleared by the staff.

"We're making progress. It doesn't help that he's so freaking gorgeous, and his smile makes me forget that I'm supposed to be mad at him. He's apologised and I feel like he's serious when he says he wants to be with me, but it'll take some time for me to trust him completely again," she admitted, watching him across the room talking to their parents. More like charming their parents.

"I just want you to be happy. If that's with him, then I support you. I've seen how you look at each other; it's obvious that there's still love there. I don't think he's been able to take his eyes off you for even a moment," Michelle said. Sure enough, when Mia glanced at him next, he was watching her.

"I'm terrified of getting hurt again. I don't think I'd survive another heartbreak," she whispered.

"More than of losing him again?" Michelle asked. "I know what I said in the past, about being from two different worlds, but you glow around him. Whether you're happy or sad or pissed off, you light up, and I've missed seeing it."

"You make me sound like a light bulb," she giggled.

"And he certainly turns you on," Michelle teased, nudging her.

"Don't be gross!" Mia swatted her sister, feeling herself go bright red.

"Sorry, I couldn't help myself, but you know I'll support you whatever you decide. Molly and I both will." Michelle kissed her cheek.

"I wouldn't want your meddling to go to waste," Mia said, as the music started. It was a pre-planned playlist, since the band wasn't meant to be playing until tomorrow night.

"I think I'm in desperate need of a dance with my wife-to-be to help digest dinner," Michelle announced. "Speaking of Molly and August, where have those two disappeared off to?"

Mia wondered if they were working on tomorrow's surprise for Michelle. She couldn't wait to see her sister's face, but her thoughts were interrupted when she saw her grandma approaching her from across the room with a cheeky grin.

"Ginny, what are you up to?" Michelle asked.

"Nothing." Ginny smirked, not meeting her eye.

"You only smile like that when you're up to no good," Mia put in.

"My dearest granddaughters, how poorly you both think of me. My heart is breaking," Ginny said, clutching her pearls. "Michelle, I would never scheme against you at your own wedding." She winked.

"That's me in the clear, then," Michelle said, standing up. "I'll leave Mia in your scheming hands."

"Don't you dare!" Mia scowled at her sister for abandoning her, but then she saw Molly on the dance floor motioning for her to join and let her go. "Just remember, I'm only letting things slide because it's your wedding. Once it's over, you owe me big time."

"I'll be happy to repay you on your big day." Michelle patted her on the top of the head before joining her future wife on the dancefloor, in the centre of the room beneath a grand, glistening chandelier. Fairy lights decorated the high beams, swinging from one to the next; against the dark wood, they created the effect of dancing beneath the night sky.

"What are you planning?" Mia narrowed her eyes at Ginny, waiting for the shoe to drop.

"Don't be so testy. You'll like this surprise. I've someone I want you to meet—"

"No, no! Absolutely no. You promised you wouldn't set me up anymore," Mia exclaimed, trying to escape, but her grandmother was quick to follow. Where the hell was August when she needed him?

"I promised that I wouldn't bring men to the bakery anymore," Ginny corrected her.

"Same thing."

"You complained I was interrupting your workday and that you were too busy, so it wasn't fair to them, since you didn't have the time to give them your undivided attention."

"So you thought Michelle's wedding would be the perfect chance to pounce?"

"Do you want to be single forever?" Ginny asked, wrapping her faux fur shawl around her shoulders, even though the fires at either end of the ballroom and the candles on the table kept the room toasty.

"Would that truly be such a terrible thing?"

"Yes, when you're doing it out of fear of having your heart broken again instead of just wanting to be alone."

"Who told you my heart was broken?" Had Michelle told Ginny about August?

"Honey, I'm not a fool. You're gorgeous, smart and talented, but you're terrible at hiding secrets. You might not want to tell me who or what happened, but I know you've been pining for someone for the last two years, and I think if you can't get over him by being single, then maybe you need to find someone else to take a chance on. Unless you have your eye on that dashing best man." Ginny fanned herself playfully. Her grandmother really couldn't take anything seriously.

Mia crossed her arms, but before she had a chance to tell her that she didn't need or want to move on from the only person who lit up her soul when he walked into a room, Ginny's eyes glinted with mischief, and Mia felt a tap on her shoulder. She turned around, surprised to see a familiar face.

"Mia, you've met Daniel before. He works in accounting," Ginny said.

"Yes, Grandma, we've met. We went to school together, and he comes by the bakery every Tuesday morning." There was no way he could be interested in her. He'd had countless opportunities to ask her out.

"I also have a soft spot for your mint chocolate cookies," Daniel added, looking rather awkward but handsome in his charcoal suit. "I'd come every day, but I'm afraid I'd get too addicted. Need to keep myself in shape." He patted his stomach; there was nothing wrong with his form. He'd been a professional skier, won every award Yule had to offer, and headed to the Outside to win what he could there before coming back home and working for his family's accounting firm.

"I'll leave you both to chat. I think my husband is looking for me," Ginny said, shuffling away, as subtle as a snowstorm in summer.

"Can I have this dance?" Daniel asked, offering his hand. Mia didn't want to turn him down flat and embarrass him, since they were standing right by the dancefloor.

"Sure – my way of apologising for my pushy grandmother. Once she gets an idea in her head, there's no stopping her. She probably saw that you frequent the bakery, and convinced herself you liked me."

"What if I do?" he said, staring down at her.

"Me or the cookies? Don't think flirting with me is getting you free baked goods."

Daniel chuckled. "That would be a nice bonus, but I have to admit that I have thought about asking you out – I just didn't want to harass you at work. I respect that you're running your business, and it wasn't the right time."

"So it wasn't my grandmother's idea?" Mia winced, not wanting to have to hurt his feelings.

"I might have been the one who offered to do her taxes if she would set us up," he confessed.

"You didn't!" She chuckled. "Trust me, she got the better deal."

"Not the smoothest move, but I thought since we were both invited to the wedding, I'd take a chance," he said, his hand settling on her waist. As nice as he was – handsome, intelligent – she felt nothing for him. He was just another customer.

"I'm flattered, but I'm already seeing someone."

Daniel frowned. "Ginny said you were single."

"It's complicated, but I don't want to lead you on when I can't get over someone else." She flushed, stepping out of his arms.

"I know when to bow away gracefully. I hope he knows how lucky he is," he said, holding his hands up.

"How lucky who is?" August interrupted, with a face like thunder.

"Whoever has won Mia's heart. He's a lucky man," Daniel said, and Mia wanted the ground to swallow her whole. August tried to conceal his smirk by rubbing his jaw, but he couldn't hide it from her. "Thank you for the dance, and I look forward to seeing you on Tuesday. I can part ways with your heart, but not with your cookies." Daniel kissed the back of her hand jokingly.

Mia chewed her lip to stop herself from laughing as August's smugness slipped away and his ears went bright red. He stepped between them quickly, forcing Daniel to drop her hand.

"Sorry to cut this short, but there's a problem with the fridge in the kitchen, and I thought you would want to check on the cake," he told Mia, who immediately panicked. Excusing herself, she hurried out of the ballroom towards the kitchen, followed closely by August. They'd fixed one issue with the band, and now the fridges weren't working?

"I think this kitchen is cursed – or the cake," she groaned, but when she stepped inside the fridge, it was working perfectly and the cake was exactly where she'd left it.

"They must've fixed it; everything seems fine with the temperature. Are you sure it was this fridge and not the fridges in the other kitchen? Because then we are really screwed for dinner tomorrow. We'd better check," Mia fretted, closing the door and turning to see August leaning against the counter.

"I lied. There's nothing wrong with the fridges." He winced, pulling at his tie.

"Why would you scare me like that?" Mia glared at him.

His words flew out in a mixture of apology and jealousy. "I came back from telling the manager about the change in the band tomorrow night, and when I got back, you were dancing with what's-his-face, and I didn't like how close he was."

"Are you serious?" She gawked at him. "You were gone for what, ten minutes, and you couldn't trust me? You were gone for two years, and I'm supposed to trust you?"

August's face fell. "That's not what I meant, and I'm truly sorry for leaving you for two years. No excuses – I fucked up. I do trust you. Do you know how scared I am of losing you? I was terrified that when I came back, someone else would've taken my place in your heart. You've no idea how lucky I feel to even get to stand within ten feet of you, but I'm terrified that luck is going to run out. That I'll lose you, that I'll blink and you'll be gone. Especially because I know I deserve it. Though I can't lie, seeing you dancing with him was a nightmare I've had over and over, of another man sweeping you off your feet."

"You're jealous?" Mia sighed.

"Yes. And possessive. I don't have any right to be, and you can dance and date and do whatever you want, but could you please only want to do it with me?"

She hadn't expected him to be so honest. "We were just dancing," she reasoned.

"*You* were just dancing. I saw the way he was looking at you."

"Daniel's a customer. Yes, he wanted to ask me out, but I turned him down."

"Why?" His head shot up, and she took his face in her hands.

"Because I couldn't lead him on when I'm in love with someone else," she confessed, unable to hide or minimise her feelings any longer.

"Really?" His brows furrowed together, like he was searching for any hint of deception in her.

"Yes," she sighed, running her hands down his chest. She loved how he squirmed under her touch. "The guy who delivers my imported ingredients is very handsome, and he gives me a great discount—"

He smothered her in a hug before she could finish.

"Stop it, you're going to get makeup on your shirt," she squealed.

"Fuck the shirt. I swear, Mia, I'm never letting you go again." He eased his grip to stare at her. "I'll spend the rest of this life and the next earning every second of your love. I promise never to hide anything from you or leave you again. A better man would let you go, but I can't, I'm not."

He kissed her lips, her cheeks, her nose, his stubble grazing her face, but she was so happy that she didn't care. Hearing the desperation in his words, she knew he meant it. She didn't want a *better* man, she wanted him, fuck-ups and all. His lips turned gentle, a lingering kiss that sealed his words like an oath.

"Are you going to come back inside and ask me to dance, or are we going to stay out here all night?" she asked.

"I don't think we'll be missed, so can I have this dance?" He bowed playfully.

"You may." She curtsied, offering her hand.

They danced through the hallway all the way back to their room, neither taking their eyes off each other.

Once inside their room, Mia pushed him up against the back of the door. He grunted upon impact, but she silenced him with her lips. Her hands on his shoulders. Her hips against his. His hands worked through her hair, undoing her bun, letting her hair cascade down her back.

"Slow down, we've got all night." August smiled against her lips and wrapped his hand around the back of her neck to regain control. She was sure he could taste her desperation on her lips. The same desperate need she'd kept bottled up for days and nights now.

"I think I've waited long enough." She grinned, sliding off his tie and ripping open his shirt. He chuckled as her lips travelled down his chest until she was on her knees, unbuckling his belt.

"Screw the foreplay, plenty of time for that later." He pulled her back to her feet, and she gasped as he gripped her thighs and lifted her. She wrapped her legs around him to brace herself, relinquishing all self-control as his lips claimed hers. Carrying her across the room, he set her on the desk and peeled off her dress until it settled around her waist.

"I know – shapewear is super sexy," Mia giggled. A satin dress showed off every lump and curve. At least she was wearing a black bodysuit with lacy panels; she'd never let him see her in the flesh-toned one she'd brought as a backup.

"You could be wearing a bin bag and still be sexy," he said, and she rolled her eyes.

He pressed his lips to her breasts, pushed up thanks to the strapless bodysuit.

Mia slid off the desk and let the dress fall to the ground.

"You've no idea how many nights I've dreamed of you, of this, of holding you again," he said, stepping back to admire her standing in her heels. His eyes ran up and down her body, making her feel exposed. It wasn't like they hadn't had sex before, but this felt different; the passion and desperation in his gaze were overwhelming.

"You're making me blush," she teased, running her hands down his chest.

"One minute." August made quick work of the rest of

his clothes and grabbed a condom, compliments of the hotel, from the drawer. While he was distracted and emboldened by his desire, she tugged off her bodysuit to surprise him. When August turned around, he found her sitting on the couch, wearing only his tie around her neck.

"I'm waiting." Mia smirked.

August moved across the room and dropped to his knees. His lips brushed her knee as he slid a hand between her legs. The pads of his fingers pressed into her bare flesh, testing and teasing. He kissed her roughly, pulling her hair to draw her closer. His control over her was absolute, and she couldn't get enough as his hands explored her body. She dug her nails into the cushioned armrests to brace herself. His mouth turned up into a grin that was so dark and full of promise, her entire face heated. All it took was his hands on her waist, and it didn't matter how much she craved him. He had all the power, along with her heart. He'd had it all this time; she just hadn't been ready to admit it.

"You've any idea how sexy you are," he mused into her ear, her body humming as his fingers travelled between her breasts, over her belly and lower, to where his fingers met sweet, soft flesh. The glint in his eyes when his fingertips met the soft centre he'd been searching for nearly undid her. She shivered, unable to control her moans as his fingers worked against her, teasing her just enough to wind her up.

"Please, August, I need you," she moaned, holding his face in her hands. The love and tenderness in his gaze made her world shatter. Heat raced down her spine as he kissed her deeply and softly until her need overwhelmed her.

Mia squealed excitedly as his hands squeezed her ass and hauled her on top of him.

"Sit," he said, gruff with desire.

She placed her knees on either side of his strong thighs on the couch and leaned over him. She'd never taken a breath so deeply in all her life as when he put a hand on her hip and guided her down to meet him. Sinking onto him, the stretch was intense, as though her body was remembering him. Her hands trembled as she gripped his shoulders, taking all of him. He shuddered, burying his face in her neck, nipping at her collarbone as his hands clenched her hipbones, moving her against him.

"Good. So fucking good," he rasped.

Her body shuddered. She wrapped her arms around his shoulders, not an inch between them, until she could feel his heart pounding against her chest.

"I'm so sorry," August said, resting his forehead against hers as he rocked his hips. "I'm yours, now and forever, and I swear I'll never leave you again, never let you doubt me again."

His confession overwhelmed her. Undid every lock she had fixed around her heart. A wave of tears spilt down her cheeks, and she was sure her makeup was a mess. He ran his thumbs roughly against her cheeks as he kissed her.

"I'm yours," she rasped, struggling to gather her words as physical sensation and emotions collided.

"You're mine," he affirmed, a soft smile of relief played on his lips, and she buried her face in his shoulder, holding onto him as though the world was trying to tear them apart. He ran his hand over the nape of her neck, rolling his hips into hers mercilessly until she wasn't sure where she ended and he began.

"Come for me," August murmured into her ear.

The sheer sound of longing in his voice spiralled her over the edge into a gasping, sobbing ecstasy. He growled low as he sped up his movements. There was so much of him, so much heat, and he didn't let up an inch as he held her hard against him, finding his own release. Their movements slowed, drawing out their pleasure until the final second. Mia collapsed against him, her flushed cheek against his sweaty shoulder as they caught their breath.

"I think you've killed me," she muttered into his neck.

"Not yet," August teased, brushing her hair over her shoulder. He kissed her collarbone. "I'm just getting started. We've got a lot of time to make up for."

Picking her up in his arms, he carried her to the bed. She wrapped her arms around his neck, resting her head against his chest.

"I do plan on being able to walk at the wedding tomorrow," she giggled as he dropped her on the bed and climbed on top of her.

"Don't worry, I'll make sure you make it down the aisle." He winked, dragging his thumb along her lower lip, and she already felt her desire for him rising again. They weren't going to get their beauty sleep before the wedding tomorrow. And being with him was worth every lost second of sleep.

Outside the small chapel in the castle gardens, Mia clutched her bouquet of wild lavender and white roses. She felt far more comfortable in the kitchen than dressed up – getting her hands on a piping bag would set her nerves right – but the cake was safely tucked away. Taking a deep breath, she smiled at her sister in her stunning champagne satin dress.

"Are you ready?" Mia squeezed her sister's hand as the other bridesmaids started to head inside the chapel. She was relieved that her lavender bridesmaid's dress had secret pockets for tissues. Michelle looked like she'd stepped right out of the 1920s, her hair pinned in waves with pearls.

Michelle smiled, fixing her long lace veil over her face. "As I'll ever be."

The music started, and Mia kissed her cheek before they headed up the stone steps, lit up with lanterns. The ends of the pews were decorated with garlands of white roses scattered with snow.

"Wait, wait," Michelle said, taking Mia's arm before it was their turn to follow the others down the aisle.

"What is it? If you want to make a run for it, we can," Mia said, earning herself a chuckle as her sister smacked her lightly on the shoulder.

"No, it's nothing like that, but there is something I've to tell you."

"And you've to tell me right now? You're about to walk down the aisle! You don't want to keep Molly waiting." Mia glanced up the aisle, not wanting to delay. The old chapel was rather chilly, even with the candles lit along the sills of the stained-glass windows.

"Since you and August disappeared last night, I take it you've both turned the page, but before I get swept up in today, I couldn't let this secret linger between us."

"Didn't we promise when I arrived that we'd have no more secrets?"

"It wasn't my secret to tell. In fact, it was Molly who confided in me, so I couldn't break her confidence, but you deserve to know," Michelle fretted.

Mia frowned. "You're starting to scare me."

"August came back to Yule," she confessed.

"What?" Mia blinked, sure that she hadn't heard right. "You mean you saw him at the engagement party? I already knew that."

"No. After his friend Cillian died, he came to see Molly, the day after the funeral."

"Okay, well, it makes sense he'd want to be around

family after losing his friend," Mia said. She'd already known he'd seen his grandparents in the last two years.

"He was a mess – just appeared on Molly's doorstep. He wanted to see you, but Molly talked him out of it."

Mia felt like she had been punched in the gut; that was only a few months after he'd disappeared. Had August not told her because he didn't want her to be upset with Molly? "Why not tell me this sooner?"

"I only found out after the engagement party, and I didn't tell you at the time because you were only getting yourself back. You were finally smiling again, and the bakery was doing so well. Given the state he was in, Molly worried it would end badly for both of you. Apparently Molly warned him to get his act together first before going to see you. When you never mentioned seeing him, she figured he had listened, but Molly didn't see him again until the engagement party. We thought, hoped, that maybe time would bring you back together, but I hope you can forgive us for interfering. Are you very angry with me? I couldn't let us walk down the aisle with this between us." Michelle squeezed her hand.

Mia shook her head. "I'm not angry. August made his own decision. You didn't know until after the fact, and Molly and I didn't know each other. If you had told me when you found out, I'd have spent months wondering why he changed his mind. I appreciate your concern and wanting to protect my heart, but this is your day, and all that matters is that you and Molly are happy. Everything else is in the past," she said, hoping to reassure her sister.

She really wasn't angry, but she wondered if he'd come to Yule just to see her, and why, if he had come so far, he had backed out at the last minute. Why hadn't he mentioned it in all their previous conversations? She shook away the thoughts, and took her sister's arm. About to walk, Michelle froze.

"What now?" Mia chuckled, tugged backwards.

"I'm really happy that you're the one giving me away," Michelle said tearfully. "We're half of the same soul, so I think it's only right that it should be you."

Mia swallowed her tears and distracted herself by fixing Michelle's veil in place. "I'm honoured, and hopefully one day you'll get to return the favour."

She took her sister's arm, trying to hold back the tears as they walked through the arched doorway. Both of them took a deep breath as the music began to play, and the guests stood as they walked down the aisle, glowing with fairy lights. It really was a fairytale moment when Mia saw Molly's face light up at the sight of Michelle; their loving gaze was undeniable. Mia couldn't help but be in awe of Molly's ability to love so ardently after all she'd lost. It felt like Mia's heart was a patchwork quilt that couldn't take another tear. But as she placed Michelle's hand on Molly's, she felt part of herself heal.

Mason Klaus, the current Santa Klaus of Yule and leader of the town council, was presiding over the wedding ceremony. It was now rare for a Klaus to marry couples, but in Yule's past, when the population was far smaller, all marriages were officiated by the sitting Klaus. Mason had offered to marry the couple in honour of the sacrifice Molly's parents had made in the mountains.

"It's an honour and privilege to stand here in front of

Mia and Molly's friends and family on this day filled with love and devotion," he said, standing between them.

Mia barely heard a word he said, because August's eyes hadn't left her since she'd walked down the aisle. This would be their last day together, their last night, and as happy as she should be for her sister, she feared losing him after only just getting him back. When the reality set in and the new year began, would he still mean all he'd said to her over the last few days?

By the time she snapped out of her fears, the rings had been exchanged. Per Yule tradition, a red ribbon bound Michelle and Molly's wrists and Yule's golden dust, a gift of luck, was sprinkled over their joined hands.

"May your new lives begin and be filled with love, luck and happiness from this day forward," Mason Klaus said, as the chapel bell rang out in celebration and the final kiss sealed the union.

Mia couldn't hold back her tears as she watched Molly and Michelle hurriedly walk down the aisle and out into the snow. She took August's arm, and they followed the couple.

"Where did you go this morning?" she asked quietly, as he'd been gone when she woke up. She figured he had gone to help Molly, as she had helped Michelle, but she'd been hoping to see him before he left.

"Your phone went off while I was in the shower," he explained.

"Oh no, I didn't even hear it! I gave the wedding planner my number in case there were any last-minute emergencies. I didn't want the brides to be disturbed."

"I answered before it disturbed you. I thought you

needed a lie-in after keeping you up so late," he whispered, and she elbowed him playfully.

"There was a flower emergency in the ballroom. Apparently, there was a miscommunication; it was meant to be white roses with lavender sprigs on the seats and tables, but the table arrangements ended up being giant bushels of lavender with only a few white roses. But we got it sorted, and after generously tipping some waiters to help the florist redo the arrangements in time for the reception, the crisis has been averted. Nothing like a last-minute surprise," he said, kissing the back of her hand.

"Speaking of surprises, I didn't know you came back to see me after Cillian's funeral," Mia said casually, and his grip on her hand tightened.

"I did. I came by the bakery, but I couldn't go in." He nodded, and she was relieved he didn't try to lie.

"Why didn't you tell me that you came by the bakery?"

"I couldn't stay away," August confessed, stopping them as they reached the doorway. "After Cillian's funeral, I just needed to see you, to know you were okay. I watched you through the window. You were wearing that pink apron with gingerbread men, and a pen was holding your hair together as you served some customers. You looked happy – content. That one look got me through months of grief. As much as I wish I had the guts to open that door, get on my knees and plead for mercy, I was a mess. The threats were getting worse back home, and I couldn't bring myself to put your life at risk because I needed you. What got me through was knowing you were safe in Yule, and I swore that once my life on the Outside was resolved, I'd come back and earn the right to stay by your side, to be the man who truly deserves to be with you. Molly and Michelle's wedding just beat me to it." His troubled gaze searched hers for any trace of anger.

"You're back now, that's all that matters." She smiled softly, and his shoulders relaxed as if he had been holding his breath.

Mia went to walk on, but he held her tightly.

"What is it?" She frowned, following his finger as it pointed to the top of the archway.

"Mistletoe." August smirked, his hands on her waist.

Mia rolled her eyes, but wrapped her arms around his neck and kissed him feverishly. He squeezed her tightly and spun her around playfully. It all felt far too good to be true.

A round of applause caught them off guard, and he put her down. They stared out at the gardens to find the brides and the rest of the wedding party clapping for them. Mia buried her face in August's chest to hide her embarrassment.

"It's about damn time," Molly called out, guiding her wife up the path back to the castle.

"Cat's out of the bag now," August said, holding Mia close.

"I think you put that mistletoe there on purpose." She swatted his chest, wondering if he'd exposed their relationship intentionally, but she didn't care; she was tired of secrets.

"I'd never." He smirked, kissing her cheek before they followed the rest of the party to the reception, hand in hand.

"Before we bring out the cake, I just want to say a few words," Mia said, trying not to stammer over her speech as her emotions threatened to take over. Michelle reached for her hand to reassure her. "I'm sure most of you can guess that Michelle is my sister, which is wild because we look nothing alike."

That earned her a small laugh, giving her the confidence to continue.

"What you might not know is that I am the eldest, by a whole four minutes. As her big sister, it was my duty to look out for her, make sure she got to school on time, and teach her to tie her shoelaces. I taught her how to ice skate, and how to drive a sleigh even though she can't be trusted to slow down on sharp corners and feeds the reindeer too many carrots. Michelle liked me to learn first, so she could learn from my mistakes, and I was more than happy to take the scraped knees and bruises. I even gave her her first haircut – sorry, Mum – and helped sneak her out of class early so she wouldn't miss her favourite cooking show. This day isn't about me, but I'm telling you these things because I wouldn't be able to hand over my other half, my partner in crime, to anyone other than Molly. Her love for Michelle since the day they met is the kind of love many of us can only hope to experience. Molly, thank you for loving my sister and bringing your light to our family. I know you'll both care for and protect each other from any challenges life throws at you, which is all I ever hoped for. Please join me in raising a glass to the brides, Michelle and Molly. I hope and pray this is only the start of your wonderful lives together."

Mia clinked her champagne flute with Michelle and Molly, who got up and hugged her tightly.

"No tears," Molly said, fighting her own.

"I hope you love the cake – so eat and drink and let's start the new year together," Mia finished, smiling like an idiot.

There was a round of applause, and Michelle beamed as the cake was brought out on the golden tray table. From her and Molly's reactions, it was everything they'd wanted. After cutting the cake together, they refrained from shoving pieces into each other's faces – because no one wants to pay to have their makeup done only to have it ruined with icing smudges.

"This is incredible. If it didn't taste so good, I would just want to keep it," Michelle said, hugging her sister tightly.

"The gingerbread's out of this world," Molly said, biting the head off one of the mini figures.

"I'm just happy you love it. I've saved an extra tier for

you to freeze so you can have it on your one-year anniversary," Mia told them.

With the cake served, Mia felt she could finally breathe. They'd managed to make it through the day without any catastrophes. Thankfully, the snow had stopped, and August had checked on the back gardens to make sure everything was set for the surprise. The band was causing the dancefloor to vibrate beneath her feet, and she loved seeing her sister so happy as Molly spun her around the dance floor. The rest of the guests were having an equally good time, as the champagne flowed and the clocked ticked down to midnight.

"Everything's ready to go. The wedding planner is going to cut the power, and the band and Molly will get out of here. I need you to get Michelle outside when the lights come back on," August said, by Mia's side.

"Okay. I'll distract Michelle, so you can grab Molly without her noticing," Mia said, enjoying their little secret mission.

August kissed her cheek and sent her off to interrupt the happy couple.

"Mind if I cut in?" Mia asked, side-eying Molly so she understood the plan, then giving August a discreet nod.

"My dancing feet could use a break. Think I'll go switch to flats," Molly said, clicking her heels before hurrying towards August.

"You may have this dance," Michelle said, offering her hand. Mia spun her around, before dipping her. "Thank you for making this weekend all the more special. The cake, putting up with sharing with August – even if I think that worked out nicely—"

Mia snorted.

"I really couldn't have done this weekend without you."

"You're not just my sister, but my best friend. Nothing in the world could've kept me away, and I'm so glad you found Molly. You both really deserve every happiness."

"I only hope you can be as happy with August."

"We're a work in progress, but I can't pretend I don't love him," Mia confessed. "He's worth the effort, and even if we have some healing to do – nothing can be cured in a weekend – I think we've the foundation to be something better. Stronger, even. This is our second chance, and I don't want to waste it."

"Well—"

The power cut out, and the music stopped. There were a few frightened yelps, but the lights shining in from the gardens quickly distracted the guests, who started to drift outside.

"What's going on?" Michelle groaned. "Why isn't the back-up generator coming on?"

"You'll see," Mia said, leading her out to the garden, lit up with lanterns and a canopy of fairy lights over the dancefloor.

"Where is the music coming from?" Michelle fretted as it started, but Mia took her hand and dragged her to where the stone square had been shovelled to make the perfect dancefloor, with heaters in every corner.

"A dancefloor under the stars? I love it. I can't believe you did this," Michelle gasped.

"I didn't do a thing." Mia pointed to the stage, where

Molly had just joined the band, August following with his guitar.

Michelle's hand went to her heart. "Oh my gosh! What is she doing? She never sings except for in the shower – she has terrible stage fright!" Her concern for her bride was adorable.

"This was her idea. You've always said she has a great voice," Mia said, "and she wanted to do something special for you."

Mia saw the tears in her twin's eyes as Molly sang Michelle's favourite song, and the rest of the guests held each other as they danced. Mia locked eyes with August and mouthed a thank you; he'd helped make this night special for them. He winked at her, and she couldn't wait to get him alone.

The band took over as Molly walked down the steps to join her bride on the dance floor. Mia thought her sister was going to crumble as she ran into Molly's arms.

"I can't believe you did that," she cried, kissing her bride and checking her over as though looking for any injuries. "Your stage fright!"

"I can't believe it either, but you always said I shouldn't hide my voice, and I wanted to be brave for you." Molly shrugged. "You gave me the courage to get up there, and now I think you owe me a dance."

"Thank you for helping her," Michelle said to August, who had just wrapped his arms around Mia's waist. It had only been a few minutes, but her body hummed, having missed his touch.

"She did it all on her own. I was just back-up," he claimed. If Mia hadn't loved him before, she was doomed now. Michelle chuckled as Molly spun her away. They really were too adorable for their own good.

"Dance with me," August said, his lips brushing Mia's. She turned in his arms and let him dip her. She shook her head, unable to contain her laughter.

"It's almost midnight," he said, as the band interrupted a song to give a ten-minute countdown warning before starting the next set. "Follow me!"

"Where are we going?" Mia giggled, lifting the ends of her dress, but she struggled to keep up as her heels caught on the cobblestones. August swept her up in his arms and carried her inside and up the staircase. They climbed out of a window on the fourth floor onto the battlements of the castle, overlooking the wedding party and the snow-covered mountains, just as the cheering crowd started the final countdown.

"I wanted us to start the New Year with the best view," August said, putting her down. He took off his jacket and slipped it over her shoulders. It smelled like him, and the lingering warmth of his body made her giddy.

Together, they stared out at the breathtaking view as they joined in on the count.

"Five."

"Four."

"Three." August pressed his lips against hers. "Just practising."

She rolled her eyes as he held her face in his hands.

"One!" Everyone cheered.

Mia wrapped her arms around August's neck, pressing her lips against his. He pulled her closer, devouring her until she couldn't breathe and the rest of the world slipped away. Snuggling close together, they watched the fireworks crackle and whistle into dark skies and burst with glistening colours.

"Happy New Year," August whispered, kissing her forehead.

"Happy New Year," Mia sighed, resting her head on his shoulder. She'd never expected this was how she'd be ending the year and starting the next, but this was the only place in the world she wanted to be – with him and her family, about to start a new adventure.

"Close your eyes and hold out your hands," Mia said, climbing back into her bed beside August at the crack of dawn, wearing his T-shirt and a Santa hat.

"I thought we were done with the blindfold," August teased, sitting up against the pillows.

"Naughty! Behave or you won't get your gift," she warned, sitting on her knees with her hands behind her back.

"I'll be good." August smirked, closing his eyes and holding out his hands.

Mia chewed her lower lip to contain her excitement. She was about to remove her hands from behind her back, but she noticed his eyelashes flutter.

"No peeking," she exclaimed.

"Sorry, it was a twitch." He squeezed them shut and let out a sigh.

"Ta-da!" She beamed, placing the gift in his hands.

"It's a scroll?" August frowned, staring at it curiously. "I was hoping it was going to be something red and lacy that would look great on the floor."

"That would be in another box." She rolled her eyes – he obviously didn't realise what she had just given him. She had been waiting months to share it, and biting her tongue hadn't been easy. She'd wanted to make sure the council of Yule approved her guardianship paperwork so she'd be able to get her Outside papers before she got his hopes up.

August reached for her, but she pushed him away playfully.

"Just open it," she chuckled, "or you're going on the naughty list and you won't get any more presents."

His puzzled expression amused her more than it should have as he removed the red ribbon and unrolled the papers.

"You got your guardianship papers?" he exclaimed, staring at the council's seal of approval on her papers – including the issue of her Outside passport and the paper trail, so that she could exist in the outside world without any suspicion. Now, if anyone, including reporters, looked into her, Yule's secret was safe. "I can't believe you didn't tell me you had applied. I know you said you were going to, but with the bakery being so busy and my grandparents giving me their bell, I didn't realise you'd already started the process." He wrapped his arms around her, suffocating her, and she couldn't contain her joy.

After a moment she leaned back, as he stared at the papers like they were going to disintegrate. "I know we've been making it work, and the bell helps, but I know how hard it is for you to keep our relationship a secret from your band, and this way, we don't have to hide."

"I don't want you to feel pressured to join me on the Outside," he reassured her. It was sweet of him, but she wanted to do this for both of them.

"There's no pressure, I know you wouldn't want me to do anything I'm not comfortable with, but now we can be seen together in public without ever having to worry. We can finally just *be*." Over the past year, he'd made the effort to spend as much time in Yule as he could and earn back her trust. It was hard not being able to be part of his world, especially when he was busy with the band, but a week didn't go by without him checking in or using his grandparents' bell to come and see her. She hadn't doubted his desire to be with her for even a second since Molly and Michelle's wedding weekend.

"You've no idea how excited I am to bring you home." He rested against the headboard, letting out a long sigh of relief. "You'll finally get to meet the guys. Phoebe's probably going to be protective at first, but she'll love you. They're all going to love you. I want more than anything for you to be part of my life, now that we have this. How do we go about introducing you to the Outside?"

The only people she'd met on the Outside so far were Axel – but only briefly, so it would be nice to get to know him better – and the band's German Shepherd, Bart; it was easy for a dog to keep their secret. Sometimes August brought him back to Yule when August didn't want to leave him home alone.

"All I have to do is check in with a guardian on the Outside every six months for the next three years, make sure I'm toeing the company line, and then I'll be cleared," Mia explained, and he nodded along, listening carefully. "Otherwise, we're good to go whenever we like. I've my bakery here, but Michelle still has her catering company, so I've put down that as my place of employment. I've hired more people for the bakery here. We'll figure it out. When you're away with the band, I'll focus on being in Yule. When we have time, we'll focus on being together, whether it's here or on the Outside. We've made it work so far, just coming and going. Now we'll have more options and flexibility, and we don't need to hide our relationship anymore."

August didn't even hesitate. "How about tomorrow?"

"I love the enthusiasm, but you want to go back to Dublin tomorrow?"

"I'd say we should go right now, but since I'm meant to be in Switzerland skiing, I think they'd wonder how I managed to get home so quickly," he explained. "But it would be great to have you join for Axel's Christmas dinner; he makes too much food every year, and it's absolute chaos. You'll love it."

Mia loved his excitement. "I've my physical passport already, so I'm good to go. I just need to pack," she said, excited to finally meet those who were so important to him – especially as his girlfriend, not a random catering woman who appeared at some of their events.

"I'll call them and tell them we're coming back. That

gives them some time to freak out about meeting you and buy you too many presents," he said, wrapping his arms around her.

"Do they know anything at all? I'm nervous about just appearing on their doorstep."

"They've suspected for a while that I've been seeing someone, since I've been disappearing more often. But they respect my privacy and don't press. Phoebe's the only one who knows for sure that there's someone, because she helped me pick out your Christmas present," he confessed, reaching into Mia's bedside table. "I was going to wait until tomorrow morning, but since we're giving gifts on Christmas Eve, this is for you." He handed her a red velvet box. "I hope you like it."

Lifting the lid, she discovered a delicate silver charm bracelet with two little charms.

"This is so pretty, I love it!" She beamed, picking it up, and August helped clasp it to her wrist. "Phoebe has great taste." She spun it around so she could see the charms. "I'll be sure to thank her."

"Hey, I deserve a little credit. I picked the charms," he said as she fiddled with a cute little cupcake hanging beside a guitar. The perfect start to a collection.

"Sorry, I shouldn't tease. I love it and I love that you consulted her. I can't wait to meet her," Mia said, crawling into his lap as he pouted.

"It's fine, you can make it up to me," he said, brushing her hair over her shoulders.

"Oh, really?"

"I believe you mentioned something about red lace?"

Grinning, Mia reached under the pillow, revealing a red lacy chemise.

"Put it on, and take off everything else," August ordered. She shivered as he kissed her shoulder and then her neck. She tilted her head, giving him better access.

"Take off everything?"

His lips brushed her ear as his hands settled on her bare thighs. "Keep the Santa hat on."

"You really are headed for the naughty list."

"If you don't want to join me, then do as I say. Lift your arms," he instructed. She didn't need to be told twice. He tugged off her T-shirt and shimmied the lacy fabric over her body.

"How do I look?" She flushed, fixing the tiny straps on her shoulders.

"As much as I want to bring you home, I don't know how I'm ever going to let you out of this bed."

Mia gasped as she suddenly found herself underneath him, his hard body pressed against hers.

"Don't make me regret giving you your present early. I've got to pack if we're going to leave today." She giggled as he ignored her and kissed every inch of her skin, making her giddy. She loved how desperate he was for her, never making her feel self-conscious.

"You've only yourself to blame." His hand travelled down her waist to squeeze her thigh as he feasted on her neck. She fisted the sheets, wishing he'd stop teasing her.

"You'll just have to make this morning count, because I refuse to give your roommates a bad impression of me by being late to Christmas dinner," she said, kissing the tip of his nose.

"We won't be late, but I'm going to make every minute count." He smirked, returning to exploring her body.

Mia wanted to argue. She needed time to buy gifts for his friends – it was against every Yule bone in her body to arrive empty-handed at Christmas. But maybe she could spare a few more minutes before they had to return to the real world.

Did you know that *How My Ex Stole New Year's* is a crossover novella connecting the **Village of Yule** series with my romantic suspense series, **Dangerous Harmonies**?

In Not Another Rockstar, you'll discover what August was doing during those two years away from Mia, and you'll meet the rest of the Brothers of Anarchy.

I've included Phoebe's first chapter to give you a sneak peek into the past...

"Phoebe Fletcher's illustrative paintings, currently featured at the exclusive Hogan Gallery, depict deeply emotional stories in a manner that speaks not only to children but the neglected inner child in every adult. We're expecting many great things from the social media-risen artist in the future."

Lena, her agent, read Phoebe the review from her phone because she was too nervous to read it herself. Phoebe tried to contain her happy squeals—best to be professional, considering how many people were gathered in the gallery to view the exhibition.

"They love the collection?" she asked, peering over Lena's shoulder. It was her first time being reviewed in the paper, and the praise felt too surreal to believe. It felt like she'd finally made it.

"Love it? There are two more paragraphs singing your praises!" Lena beamed, earning a few stares from those around them. "The review has been posted all over social media. Be prepared to be very busy."

"I feel like I can finally breathe again, after months of

stressing about all this. I can't believe they love it! I'm so glad I left the commission form open on my website." Phoebe couldn't wait to get home and check if she had any new commissions or print orders.

She took a deep breath and resisted the urge to burst out in a fit of joy-filled laughter. Probably better not to look like she'd lost her mind, if she wanted these people to purchase her art.

"Has Cillian seen this? When is he getting here?" Lena asked the dreaded question.

She read Phoebe's hesitation in an instant.

"Cillian hasn't turned up? You've been showing for a week, and he couldn't make it for one night? Are you serious?" she whispered as Phoebe placed a red dot on another sold painting.

She'd been worried about the price putting people off, but Lena had informed her at the start of the night that three of her largest paintings had sold to one collector at asking. The best part about having an agent was that she did all the price negotiating. Phoebe was terrible at pricing—she'd give everything away for free if she could.

"After so many years of struggling, I have a sell-out show and an agent to celebrate my success with. Please let's just bask in this moment?" Phoebe pleaded. "Do I want him here? Yes, but nothing can dull my shine right now. I've a sneaking suspicion that Cillian bought the three paintings since he couldn't make it. He mentioned wanting to purchase some art to decorate the villa in Italy."

"You're right. I shouldn't think the worst of him. I won't bring him up again, but you shouldn't let him get away with not being here for you. How many times have you made sacrifices to be at one of his shows or be there to support him?" Lena offered her a glass of sparkling water, since she didn't drink while working.

Phoebe clinked her long, manicured nails against the glass to ease her nerves. She'd had her nails done for the first time for the show, since they were usually stained with paint. Given all the hands she'd be shaking, she wanted to make a good impression—and give her hands a treat for all the hard work they'd done to bring her to this point in her career.

"It's the band's first stadium tour. Him missing one exhibition isn't the end of the world," Phoebe reasoned. She hated to be the girl who was always defending her absentee boyfriend, but she'd been with him long before he was a famous rockstar and understood the stress he was under.

"Judging by how this exhibition has gone, and the beaming faces of the gallery owners, it won't be your last show here," Lena said with a wink.

Even if exhibitions were more stressful than selling prints online, it was great to see the collection appreciated by so many in person.

"He wanted to be here, but he has a show in Munich tomorrow. I couldn't ask him to fly home for my last night. I had no expectations that he'd be here," Phoebe said, organising her remaining prints at the front of the gallery. It was awfully hot despite the late hour, and with the door opening and closing, it was nice to get a breath of fresh air. "The same way he didn't expect me to be at his London show last week because I was getting everything ready for the exhibition." Phoebe tucked a strand of her cropped lilac hair behind her ear as the draught by the door caused some strands to stick to her lip gloss.

"That's different," Lena countered, taking a salmon puff from a passing tray of hors d'oeuvres. "You've gone to countless concerts, and this is your first big exhibition."

Phoebe knew Lena didn't like her fiancé. They'd met briefly before Cillian left for the tour months back, but they hadn't clicked, and his lack of support since hadn't helped. Not that she needed them to get along. Lena was her agent first and friend second, and she was always professional.

"We're in this fabulous gallery, surrounded by fabulously creative minds, and celebrating my sell-out exhibition. Please just be ridiculously happy for me." Phoebe put out some more cards with her commission details, trying not to let Lena's concerns ruin her buzz. "Tomorrow, when you wake up hungover and I drag you to an early-riser yoga class, you can bitch as much as you want about his failures as a boyfriend."

Fiancé, Phoebe corrected herself. The ring on her finger, an obscenely large diamond that wasn't her style, glared up at her, but his heart was in the right place. They hadn't grown up with much, so he tended to overcompensate. At twenty-six, she hadn't been expecting a proposal. Her art career was taking off, and with Cillian being away for months with his band, Brothers of Anarchy, it felt crazy to think about planning a wedding.

"Fine, I'll stop." Lena gave in. "I'm ridiculously happy for you. With all the money you've made tonight, you'll be able to stop temping."

Lena was the only person Phoebe knew who loved her desk job, though she was rarely at her desk. Public relations meant she spent most of her time wining and dining, attending openings and premieres of the clients she managed.

"You'll be happy to hear I handed in my notice this morning. I'm officially a full-time artist," Phoebe said, still in disbelief. "I didn't have much of a choice, since you've already booked three more exhibitions next year." In the meantime, Phoebe hoped the royalties from this show, commissions and her website sales would keep her comfortable. Once the rent was covered and she could paint all day, she didn't care.

"I'll cheers to that! I'm sure your mum and dad are so proud of you. I didn't see them around?" Lena glanced around the busy studio, alive with small talk. Phoebe illustrated emotions as characters, with scenes to match. She loved listening to what people thought, and seeing if they could figure out what emotion each painting depicted.

"You already missed them. They were some of the first to arrive, but with Dad's bad hip they couldn't stay long," she said.

Just that morning, she'd paid them back for the two years of art school she'd attended. Her professors had called her work childish and doubted she'd ever be a 'real' artist. When she'd decided to drop out after two years, her parents never doubted her decision.

Phoebe had the internet to thank for making her a success. She'd started with small prints, but seeing the large canvases on the walls felt like coming home. For an extra dash of petty, she'd sent some of her professors invites to the opening—which went unanswered.

"I'll have to catch them next time," Lena said. "Getting back to the sunrise yoga, why do we have to get up at the crack of dawn? Why don't we have a late brunch and then go to an afternoon class like regular people?" she suggested, touching up her red lipstick. "I think celebrating should come with a long lie-in."

Lena was blessed with genes that allowed her to remain trim without having to exercise, whereas Phoebe only had to look at a dessert and her body would decide to hold onto it for life. That didn't stop her from loving her sweet treats; she'd learnt to love her curves after years of too much exercise and obsessing over 'good' and 'bad' foods. It did nothing but ruin her mental health, and what's wrong with being pear shaped? Pears are juicy and delicious.

"Because I've a flight to Munich in the afternoon," Phoebe admitted, as her phone vibrated in the pocket of her black midi dress. *Is there anything better than a dress with pockets?*

She hoped it was Cillian. Instead, it was her brother, Nick, the guitarist of Brothers of Anarchy or B.O.A for short, telling her he'd left her ticket for their concert at the hotel she'd booked last minute.

"I should've known that he'd make you go to him," Lena said, when Phoebe explained what was going on. "You haven't seen him since he proposed." Lena's moaning was interrupted by a couple asking to buy a print of an illustrated flowerpot with a terrible scowl and flaming petals. Phoebe tried not to laugh as Lena was forced into silence. The customers finished congratulating her before leaving with their purchase. Once they were out the door, Phoebe worried Lena was going to explode as she turned the same shade as her auburn hair.

"He doesn't even know I'm coming—it's a surprise," Phoebe explained. "With the exhibit over, I finally have some time before I have to work on my next collection. I want to spend as much time with him as I can, maybe start planning the wedding. I was thinking Italy, something super small at the villa where he proposed." She was getting carried away, but they had to start planning at some point and her Pinterest board was getting crowded with ideas.

"Italy is a beautiful idea, but there's no rush. You've only been engaged a few months," Lena said, always erring on the side of caution.

"I'm not saying I'm going to fly off tomorrow and elope." Phoebe tried to act as though she hadn't considered it. She'd never been to Vegas, and with their busy schedules, it was an option. If they eloped, they wouldn't have to worry about the press.

She doubted Cillian's fans would be happy with his engagement. It didn't matter that they'd been together since they were fourteen, an engaged rockstar wasn't as sexy as someone attainable. Phoebe did her best to keep her relationship away from her social media; she only posted about her art and the process that went into it. She liked to keep her private life private. But with Cillian and her brother being in one of the world's biggest bands, it was hard to hide in the shadows.

"You'd better not! But if you do, please call me. It'd

break my heart not to be there!" Lena gave her a tight squeeze.

"I promise not to get married without you."

As much as she loved the idea of a private ceremony, having Lena by her side felt equally important. She struggled for years to find a trustworthy agent, but she and Lena had been fast friends since they met at an art show last year. Any time she doubted herself, Lena would (metaphorically) slap some sense into her.

"Thank you, and since you promise not to elope, I suppose I can join you at the crack of dawn." Lena released her and put down her glass of champagne.

"I'll bring you a latte with an extra shot," Phoebe promised as they headed over to a group of guests.

The exhibition wouldn't go on much longer now that most of the paintings were sold, but she wanted to do some more mingling to thank everyone for attending.

"Better make it two extra shots!" Lena grabbed another glass of champagne. "Also, I purchased a painting for my parents. They fell in love with the breakfast scene I sent them. It'll go perfectly in their cottage kitchen."

Phoebe stared at her wide-eyed. "You didn't! I would've given it to you. Or made a copy for them!"

"Of course I did." Lena blew her a kiss. "My best friend and client is a sell-out artist, it's my duty to support you."

Phoebe couldn't argue as they joined the other guests, but she reminded herself to buy Lena a large coffee and her favourite chocolate croissant in the morning.

Continue Reading...

ACKNOWLEDGEMENTS

Thank you so much for reading Mia and August's story! I've to start by saying thank you to my dear friend and fabulous editor, Emma. I sprung the idea of a Yule Novella on her at the **VERY** last minute, and as always, she agreed to help with my crazy idea. Writing and publishing wouldn't be as fun without her.

To my beautiful readers, thank you so much for all the love and encouragement you've shown the Village of Yule for the past few years. It doesn't feel like Christmas anymore without a trip to the North Pole with you. I wouldn't be able to do what I love without the love you give my stories. Every share, comment, review, fabulous video or photo brightens my world. Thank you for letting me live my dream, and I don't take a single one of you for granted.

There are *many* more trips to Yule to come, and I promise to save you a seat on the sleigh!

The Naughty or Nice Clause

VILLAGE OF YULE

KATE CALLAGHAN

When Lyla's father retired as CEO of the toy company which has been in their family for generations, she was meant to receive his shares. Instead, she discovers the company is bankrupt and her father has given her shares to Mason Klaus, an investor known in the corporate world for his cold and callous nature. Much to Lyla's frustration, her only option is to run the company with him, despite their evident loathing for one another.

When Mason cancels the annual Christmas party, Lyla throws it anyway – only for the event of the season to result in a terrible fire. With the offices and Lyla's credibility ruined, Mason offers her a deal: he'll forget her part in the disaster, but she must join his family for the twelve days of their Christmas holidays.

Taken to a fantastical winter wonderland, Lyla hopes that she might discover some of the secrets Mr Klaus is hiding, and maybe even a way to get her company back. However, when Mason introduces her to the secret village as his fiancée, she is horrified to realise she has no choice but to go along with the pretence – because the cost of bringing an outsider to their magical land is far too high.

Can Lyla resist the devilishly handsome Mr Klaus and the enchanting village to win back her company, or will she give into temptation?

Read Me

JOIN THE MAILING LIST

Receive your **FREE** copy of Will and Juliet's story, Tis The Season For Secrets, by joining my mailing list.

Tropes & Themes
One Night Stand
Winter Wonderland
Family Secrets
Forced Proximity
Bodyguard X Editor

Sign Up To Be The First To Hear About:
- Advanced Release Copies
- Cover Reveals
- Teasers & More

ABOUT THE AUTHOR

Kate Callaghan is an Irish author who writes adult fantasy, romantic suspense, and feel-good Christmas romance. She's the creator of the Hellish Fairytale series, blending dark magic and intrigue, as well as festive romcoms like The Naughty or Nice Clause. Whether she's spinning tales of dangerous love or cosy holiday magic, you'll find her in a Dublin café with an iced coffee, plotting her next twist.

instagram.com/katecallaghanwriter
youtube.com/@katecallaghanwriter
tiktok.com/@katecallaghanwriter
bookbub.com/authors/kate-callaghan

www.ingramcontent.com/pod-product-compliance
Lightning Source LLC
Chambersburg PA
CBHW010342170726
48283CB00009B/2926